Wade Beauchamp

Scream If You Wanna Go Faster

Ink Smith Publishing
www.ink-smith.com

Scream If You Wanna Go Faster

This is a work of fiction. Names, characters, places and incidents either are products of the author's imagination or are used fictitiously. Any resemblance to actual events or locales or persons, living or dead, is entirely coincidental. Except for the really bitchin' parts. Some of that stuff actually sort of happened.

Front and back cover illustrations by Wade Beauchamp

Cover design by Adam Casey

Printed in the U.S.A

ISBN: 978-1-939156-04-4

Lyrics from the song "Zip City" are used with permission. Words and music by Mike Cooley and Drive-By Truckers © 2001. All rights reserved. Used by permission of Mike Cooley and Red Light Management.

Wade Beauchamp

For Ronda, Lillie, Paul and Dad

"I get ten miles to the gallon. I ain't got no good intentions"

- Mike Cooley

Contents

1963
Prologue

On April 29, 1959, Ford Motor Company's 50 millionth car rolled off the assembly line in Lorain, Ohio. It was a Galaxie 500 4-door sedan. White with three-tone gold, black and white interior. 292 cubic inch V8, 200 horsepower. The car travelled coast to coast, taking part in transcontinental races, various promotional appearances and was eventually donated to the Henry Ford Museum.

Four years later, at Atlanta Assembly in Hapeville, Georgia, Ford built its 60 millionth car. A 1963½ Galaxie 500 XL Sport Roof, Rangoon Red on black, Z-code 390, 4-speed transmission. There was no fanfare, no VIPs. No one even noticed. With the exception of Frank Lukon.

Frank had worked at Atlanta Assembly since he got back home from Korea. It was his job to bolt on those big chrome bumpers. Frank couldn't read or write, but he knew how to work.

Frank silently and solemnly thanked every bumper he bolted for the food they put on his family's table and the roof they kept over their head.

The Galaxie that Frank helped build was driven onto a transport and hauled up brand new Interstates 85 and 40 to Winston-Salem, NC, where it found a temporary home on the lot of Parkway Ford. Glen Smith cashed the commission check he got from selling the car and spent the money on a fifth of J&B and a night at the Holiday Inn for him and his mistress.

Glen had sold the car to Freddie Hudspeth, a surveyor from Lewisville who drove the car up and down the state highways, rural routes and two-rut washboard dirt roads of Forsyth, Yadkin, Surry and Stokes Counties for seven years and 141,970 miles. He drove it until his son's sixteenth birthday, at which point he drove back down to Parkway Ford and bought a new 1969 LTD. (351 Windsor, 2-barrel. He had learned his lesson with the Galaxie's thirsty 390.)

After Freddie Hudspeth, Jr. ("Fadie" to his friends and family) blew out the candles, his father gave the boy a big hug and dangled the keys above his son's upturned palm until Fadie promised he would spend the next two summers carrying the theodolite and tripod into the woods, across ditches, creeks, swamps and the private property of suspicious and irritable land owners.

In his sixteenth year on this Earth, Fadie Hudspeth fell desperately in love with two things: Veronica Sue Everly from his

10th grade Social Studies class, and his 1963½ Ford Galaxie 500 XL Sport Roof.

1972

American Butterflies

1

"Goddamn, she's pretty," Boggs says to me.

I had been scanning the skies over U-Tapao Air Base, crisscrossed with contrails, marveling at how these clouds looked exactly like the ones on the opposite side of the globe.

"You say that every time, Boggs. You know that, right?"

"Well, it's the goddamn truth every time."

"Don't say 'goddamn'. The last thing we need about now is the Almighty bearing a grudge."

"Damn, Fadie, don't you know we got the Almighty on our side? Tricky Dick hisself says so." Boggs punches me on the arm hard enough to break my stride. "Besides, *Ronnie Baby's* pretty almighty herself. Just ask those gooks at Van Dien."

Boggs starts talking about what it must have looked like to be on the ground when our bombs hit the factories and all those ball bearings got blasted into the air. For a minute I try picture to it in my head: the concussive impacts of each detonation, the shockwaves expanding like ripples on a pond, so rapidly that the

10

water vapor in the air condenses into fleeting halos. I picture the fireballs and hurricanes of dust and smoke and debris, and millions and millions of shiny, tiny metal spheres launched airborne like rice at a wedding. Then Boggs starts talking about the bodies and I stop listening.

We always walk to her en masse, all six of us. Across the tarmac, the jungle is far enough away to look like the honeysuckle and pines of home, not the bamboo and mangroves of Thailand. Boggs is the only one talking, as usual. I have no idea what the others think about on our walk. The mission, maybe. Their mamas. Their girlfriends. What heaven is like. I don't know. Me, all I can think about is Veronica. I glance up at her, perched on the nose of our silver plane. She wears a tiny leather vest, the collar trimmed with fur, hanging unzipped in front, parted by the most perfect pair of tits I've ever seen. A pair of bombardier's goggles are atop her head, pushing back windswept raven locks. Around her hourglass waist hangs a gun belt of tanned rawhide, the bullet loops fully stocked, a gleaming, pearl-handled six-shooter in the holster. Otherwise she's completely naked, sitting pretty on the nose of our B-52D Stratofortress, her breasts pointing the way toward North Vietnam. She's flashing that mega-watt smile and ready with an All-American wink for Charlie.

Boggs had wanted to name our B-52 after Veronica from the moment he first saw her picture in my wallet. He could've named the plane whatever he wanted; as our pilot, that was his right. But Boggs being Boggs, he'd pulled me aside and asked if

11

I'd mind the bomber being named after my girl. He said he'd name it after his own girl but he was sure she was screwing around on him back home. And besides, he had said, she wasn't nearly as pretty as Veronica. Boggs took the rest of the crew out for a beer and asked for their blessing. He made me pass around the snapshot of Veronica and they all agreed on the spot we should be flying the *Ronnie Baby*.

We actually flew our first two missions without Ronnie. That second run was the time we lost Robert. As soon as we touched down in U-Tapao, Boggs swore we weren't going back up again until Ronnie was painted on the plane. Lee Atwater did it. He did practically all the nose art for the 7 AF. Only took him one afternoon, even with me and Boggs watching over his shoulder the whole time, making sure he got the eyelashes just right, telling him that the burgundy of Ronnie's lips was a little deeper; her eyes a lighter shade of blue, her ass a little rounder. She took up a panel and a half, a line of rivets running right across the crest of her breasts. Over her head in an arching script, it read: *Ronnie Baby*. For nineteen missions now, Ronnie's led us into the heart of North Vietnam and back again, those perfect tits showing the way.

I make my way to the *Ronnie Baby* and wait my turn to climb in. I look up at Veronica and wink back. I close my eyes for just a second and get a flash of her body pressed against mine.

"Fadie! Get your ass on the plane!" I hear Boggs holler.

I tell Veronica I'll see her after we've dropped the bombs. I'll see her soon. It's enough to get me on that goddamned plane.

***

Permanence is the illusion of every generation. Somebody famous said that, I'm pretty sure. Had you told me in 1969 that in four short years Detroit's Big Three would be castrated by a veritable alphabet of enemies – OPEC, NHTSC, OSHA, EPA – I would have called you crazy. In 1969, Detroit was quite literally firing on all eight cylinders. The tweed Fifties had finally ebbed against Rayon shores in 1962, when all but the last of the Futurama fins and afterburner taillights disappeared. The Pontiac GTO and the Ford Mustang had kicked open the doors of the youth market and the Big Three were reaching the crescendo of a twenty-year horsepower arms race. They gave us machines with names like Road Runner Superbird, Cyclone Spoiler II, Stage 1 GS, and Torino Talladega (an odd pairing of Italy and Alabama). Gone were the yacht-like proportions and performance of the decade prior. Gone were the flying ladies on the hoods and acres of chrome, blown away by GT stripes, hood scoops and miniskirts. By the time I entered my senior year of high school in the fall of 1969, the manufacturers had abolished their self-imposed displacement limits and 1970 models boasted power plants that easily broke the old 400 cubic inch mandate. 426 Hemis, 428 Cobra Jets, 454 LS6s battled stoplight to stoplight on the boulevards and backstreets with nothing less than the hearts and minds of America's teenagers at stake.

13

How many nights had I lain awake with those cars howling down the alleys of my mind, their imagined tire-screeches echoing in my head? How many afternoons had those machines raced down the margins of my college-ruled spiral notebooks while Mrs. Zimmer rambled aimlessly about hypotenuses and parabolas? By the end of the school year, my book bag bulged with dog-eared and tattered copies of *Car Craft* and *Hot Rod,* and my three-ring binder was tattooed with ballpoint doodles of checkered flag fender badges and chrome avatars of mustangs and impalas, galloping across proclamations of cubic-inch displacement. I yearned for those cars. I ached for them. But I knew nothing like a Boss 429 or Shelby GT500 was remotely within the realm of possibility. Still, for a while that summer I had naïvely allowed myself to hope that a Mustang Fastback would be sitting in the driveway on my sixteenth birthday, a hot little 302 under the hood.

What I got instead was my Old Man's worn-out Galaxie. I hated it. Its red paint was pocked-marked from the miles of gravel roads he'd traversed in the thing. The front seat was a vinyl slab of a bench seat you'd slide halfway across if you dared take a turn too fast. The trunk lid alone looked as long as a lot of new cars. The 390 under the hood was no slouch, but the three 2-barrel carbs were a monster to keep tuned. Worst of all – its most grievous offense – was the fact that it wasn't a muscle car. Not my definition of one, anyhow. It was my father's car. His work car, at that. A big, plain sedan perfectly suited for a 54-year man who wore horn-rimmed glasses and short-sleeve dress shirts. The

14

salt in the wound was the fact that I'd had to agree to work for him over my next two summer vacations in return for the privilege of driving of what amounted to a pair of wingtips on wheels.

There was one other thing, too: I was dead wrong. The second day I drove it to school, Veronica Everly asked me for a ride to lunch. The sight of her slipping onto the passenger's side of that bench, her slate-colored wool skirt slipping over her knees for the fleetest of moments, her alabaster thighs sliding across my vinyl, is forever seared into my memory. She blushed, smiled, and tugged her skirt back down. We went to the Triangle and she told me she liked my car.

Veronica needed a ride to lunch again the next week. Twice the week after that. By October she was riding with me every day, in spite of the protests from her friends. It took me until second semester but she said yes when I asked her if she wanted to go to the movies. We went to see *Butch Cassidy and the Sundance Kid* and on the way home Kent Butner challenged me to race his '68 Z28 to the next stoplight, "That is," he grinned, "Unless you're scared of wrecking your grandma's car." We beat Kent by two car-lengths and Veronica said she loved my car. The adrenaline of the race was making my hands tremble so I kept them clamped to the steering wheel when I asked if I could kiss her. We were doing ninety.

"Right here?" she'd said.

"Right here and now."

Scream If You Wanna Go Faster

***

The Vietcong attacks always begin without any Vietcong. Well, the Vietcong are there alright, it's just that we can't see them. Which has always struck me as a little chickenshit. Then again, I suppose the same thing could be said of us, 129 B-52D Stratofortresses, in formation seven miles above the Earth. But give me MiGs any day over SAMs. At least we can see those bastards. At least then we can fight back.

From my position in the tail gunner turret I watch a pair of SAMs streak skyward from the Yen Vien storage complex 40,000 feet below. Coils of white smoke trail from them, tracing back to the verdant canopy of the jungle. As soon as I'd seen them I called for a break left and Boggs responded instantly. These wouldn't have hit us either way. The close ones arc by with a muffled screech, barely audible over the mind-numbing drone of eight Pratt & Whitney J57 turbojets. The really close ones sound like howler monkeys, making the glass tremble as they shriek past. But these aren't close ones.

The metal womb of the B-52's turret feels even tighter than usual, the dead-end of a narrow tunnel, bristling with toggles and dials. Arteries of wire and cable snake all around. The radar scope gazes at me like a Cyclops, just above the maw of the optical sights. I scan the sky through armored glass, my four .50 caliber machine guns looking in whichever direction I do. But my guns and I are just spectators at this point. I say two prayers: *Please,*

16

Boggs. Get us through this, and *Please, God. Let me see Veronica one more time*. And just as quickly I make an addendum to the latter. *And my car, God. Let me see my car one more time.*

Two planes over, a SAM rips into an engine, exploding into a sooty ball of flame and yanking me back into the present. The bomber staggers and then her wing just folds up and she goes straight down, trailing a plume of smoke, shedding pieces of metal and burning fuel. Our plane shudders from the concussion of the blast, the shrapnel flying against the hull like a thousand ice picks. And for a few seconds I feel a little better, going with the logic that we won't be due for a close call for while.

I can't see them as our bombs fall free but I feel the plane lurch upward and hear her engines break into full-throttle roar, then the ironically comforting "Bomb's away" from Boggs over the intercom. Seventy thousand pounds of metal and explosive shrieking out of the sky. Bye-bye, Charlie. The formation turns west to escape the SAMs and head back to base. Boggs has answered my prayer again. Now if God can live up to His end of the bargain.

Soon the intercom begins to crackle with old jokes that seem funnier than ever. Below us the sky has become overcast, obscuring that god-awful piece of Earth, and we seem to be hovering over a vast sea of cotton stretching from horizon to horizon. There's a sense of movement, but not of forward motion, like we're shiny model airplanes hung from the ceiling of heaven.

And just like that I leave the here and now behind. Instead of being balled into the tail gunner turret of a B-52D

Stratofortress, I'm lying on my bed with Veronica. The oxygen from my mask becomes a warm autumn breeze through my window, carrying on it Veronica's Jean Naté. She's making fun of me because I haven't changed my bedroom since I was 12-years old. We lie on the OK Corral sheets, under the shelf over my headboard that still holds my Little League trophies. She laughs when she sees "Freddie" on the nameplate and I explain that when I was little I couldn't pronounce my own name. Veronica had brought over her Jimi Hendrix and Big Brother and the Holding Company records; she made me quit playing *At Folsom Prison* and put on *Electric Ladyland*, then *Cheap Thrills,* instead. I didn't understand either of them, but I understood Veronica. In less than a year, Jimi and Janis would both be dead.

Veronica stares up at the 1/48 scale B-17G Flying Fortress that dangles from 12-pound test fishing line above us.

"Do you think she's pretty, Fadie?" she asks.

"Not as pretty as the Mustang," I say, pointing to the silver P-51 suspended a few feet over.

"I wasn't talking about the plane. I meant her." Veronica points to the B-17's nose, to a yellowed and peeling decal of a half-naked pin-up girl straddling a fat bomb, *Auf Wiedersehen!* in arcing script above her.

"Not as pretty as you."

She helps me wash the car, wearing those little white shorts. Momma never said anything about them, but I know she hated those shorts. I watch Veronica push that sudsy sponge all over the Galaxie, sliding it down the fenders, leaving a trail of

18

rainbow-colored foam slipping down the cherry red paint. She's gorgeous, her body perfectly shaped, all swells and curves, every inch reflecting sunlight. And Veronica is just as beautiful. My two beautiful girls.

We stretch out on the warm hood and let the sun dry our bodies as we listen to the yellow jackets buzz all around the scuppernong vines. Veronica listens as I tell her my plans for the Galaxie: American Butterfly mags, Edelbrock high-rise intake, Doug Thorley headers. She has no idea what any of it means, but she listens just the same. We eat grapes and watch the sun go down and talk about how nice it's going to be when we can say goodnight and I won't have to drive her home. Those nights were like lightning bugs, lit up for a second and then vanished into the dark under the pecan trees, gone from that spot and flashing again just out of arm's length.

Momma was peering through the Venetian blinds of her bedroom, watching for me when I got back from taking Veronica home that night. On the kitchen table was an opened letter that read, *Selective Service System. Order To Report for Induction.* It said for me to bring my glasses and proof of marriage, if I had either. It told me to bring a physician's certificate describing any physical or mental conditions I had that might disqualify me from serving. They said to bring enough clean clothes for 8 days and enough money for a month. I had none of those things.

As we fly north of Hanoi, we're alerted to fighters in the area. Within minutes comes the all too familiar "Bandits, nine o'clock high" from the top. I can hear Tim open fire, Henry in the

19

right turret does the same, then the unmistakable sound of a MiG-21 shrieking past us at 800 miles per hour. I swing my twin .50s around but not fast enough. I watch helplessly as the fighter descends until he's no more than a black speck against the clouds. He banks and realigns himself for another run on a different B-52.

The entire plane suddenly bucks. I can hear Boggs saying the Number Three engine has been hit. I wheel my turret around and see the engine, belching flame and smoke. The entire plane is trembling. More bandits are called, five o'clock, and this time I'm ready. I swing around and see them: three MiGs, bearing down hard. I see the orange flashes of their cannons and hear the shells zipping past our fuselage. Closer. Two break high, the other low. I frame the low one in my sights; follow him for a split second. Time freezes as I squeeze down my firing buttons.

The .50s roar in anger, spitting shells and filling my turret with heat and spent casings. The MiG bursts into flame, cartwheeling in midair and plummeting out of the sky like a shredded kite. The smoke from my guns fills my chest and my shoulders lift. The sky seems to loom even larger. I think about Veronica, out there on our nose, naked in a minus-sixty degree headwind, still smiling, still winking. I squeeze my eyes shut and forget here: the plane, the bombs, the guns. And the swarming MiGs are little more than tumbling leaves. It's autumn and we're driving. I hear the tires slapping at the pavement, the constant hum of the engine, the song of Veronica's laughter. I see the vermillion smears of the landscape blurring by, the mirror-red of the hood, sunlight on chrome. The wind rushes in and Veronica's hair whips all around like brunette flames. Almost home, baby.

Everyone's checking in – Radio OK, Left Waist OK, Tail OK... We're all okay. She's got some damage. Number Three engine gone, of course, and the skin is peeled back, revealing the wing struts. But otherwise, she's okay. We've fallen below and behind the formation, they can't wait for us. But we're okay. If this is all we get...

"Bandits at seven o'clock high," comes the call. I get ready again. I scan the sky and see the looming silhouettes of our pursuers, my fingers tightening on my triggers just as I realize they're F-4 Phantom IIs scattering the remaining MiGs. The Phantoms glint in the sunlight as they streak by us. The only thing between us and base now is atmosphere and distance.

I'm paranoid for the first half hour after we lose the formation. I worry over every sound *Ronnie Baby* makes. I hear a rattle or knock and wonder what's going on. Is that a normal sound? Have I heard that before? Is the wing coming off? Slowly I let it sink in that we're going to make it. Again.

We touch down in U-Tapao. Boggs examines our busted wing and there's a look on his face that lets me know it's a lot worse than he realized.

I take a minute to look at *Ronnie Baby*, at rest, nose pointing skyward, like she's looking back at it wistfully, ready to go again.

"Ronnie got us home again, didn't she, Al?" he says, as he clamps an arm around me and drags me toward the hangar.

Scream If You Wanna Go Faster

She sure did.

1974
Triggers

At some point every day something triggers my memory and I think about him. From the day he got the letter, I began going about my daily life imagining how it would feel if he never came back. Whatever it was I was doing at the time, whether it was folding towels, going to the bank, stopping for gas, whatever. I tried on every possible activity, every potential situation I could think of, and I would ask myself, how will it feel to be doing this after my son is gone?

Most days it's accidental, his memory turning up unexpectedly. Like when I go get my medicine at Gordon Manor Pharmacy and pass the spinner rack where he used to stand and flip wide-eyed through issues of *G.I. Combat* and *Sgt. Rock*, or the lunch counter where we'd sit and I'd buy him a hot dog if my prescription wasn't ready yet. Or the plastic model section where he'd beg for that same 1940 Ford Coupe kit I'd gotten him time and time again, only to have him accidentally splatter lighter fluid on the windshield or get a run in the paint, and then he'd beg for a new kit so he could start fresh.

Every week, when I see Bessie Everly at the grocery store, I think of him. I wonder if Mrs. Everly knows how important her daughter was to Fadie. I want to tell her how sweet Veronica was. I want to tell her I had hoped that one day my son and her daughter would be married. I want to tell her that I'm sure, that when it got bad over there, the thought of Veronica had helped Fadie go someplace nicer in his head. I want to tell her, but I can't even make eye contact with her.

I think about him whenever Fred and I sit at our kitchen table and can't find anything to talk about. I remember the three of us sitting around that table the night Fadie got his letter, and all of us holding hands and praying. I remember Fred and I being so proud and brave in front of Fadie but then crying till dawn after Fadie went to bed.

The smell of a sidewalk when a shower begins. The dark wet spots slowly displacing the lighter dry areas, the randomness of the pattern of the raindrops, makes me think of Fadie flying through the air in that airplane as flak turned the sky into a cobweb of smoky black blotches.

Whenever Major tries to nudge open Fadie's bedroom door but can't because it's locked, then he just lies down at the door and whines.

Whenever they call out 'B'-anything at bingo night, but especially when they call out B-52.

Whenever Fred looks at me with those blue eyes he gave Fadie.

The smell of blown-out birthday candles.

Anytime I see an Oriental person. I don't even know what a Vietnamese looks like, if they look different from the Koreans that Fred killed or the Japs my daddy killed. And I don't care.

Whenever I smell a diesel engine, I think of the last time I saw him, waving from the window of that bus.

Whenever someone drops a utensil at dinner, I remember how I fumbled with my silverware at dinner after Fred and I had dropped Fadie off. I was suddenly famished; I don't think I had eaten anything that day, too nervous. And my hands were trembling, all the fear and dread and sorrow that I had suppressed flooded through my body and I couldn't even hold my fork.

Whenever the clock over the stove is on 4:23pm, I remember the knock on my door that came that one afternoon. I had known somehow. I remember the paralyzing fear that washed over me. Whenever I open my front door, I remember the courage I had summoned to do it that day.

I think of him every time I go out to the clothesline and I catch a glimpse of the Galaxie out of the corner of my eye, when the bumper catches the sun. Fred had parked it out in the shed and for the most part I was able to ignore it. But people started stopping by every now and then and asking if it was for sale, which it most certainly is not. We've slowly started stacking stuff on top of it – the cardboard tray I use to gather walnuts, stacks of the *Journal* and *Sentinel* tied up with string, wooden crates full of those glass pop bottles Fred used to collect – to the point that I just about can't see it anymore.

For a long time, whenever I thought of heaven, or something like it, I tried my hardest to believe in it. And I would remember something Fred once told me that he and Fadie would talk about when they were surveying. When Fred would send Fadie tromping off down some two-hundred foot property line, Fred would call after Fadie and ask him if he thought he had walked half the way yet. Then he'd call out to him and ask if he'd walked half of what was left, all the way until Fadie got to the end of the line. When Fadie would return, Fred would ask him how he ever got where he was going if he only kept cutting the remaining distance in half. Whenever I think of heaven, I like to think that somewhere Fadie is still cutting that distance in half.

1981
Nowhere Fast

The first place my big brother ever drove us after getting his driver's license was Stratford Road. Mom had picked him up early from school and taken him in her piss-yellow '76 Ford Elite down to the Highway Patrol station to take the test. Despite a half-mile of hood to peer over and a steering wheel that was about as responsive as a butter churn, Dorsey passed. He brought Mom home, picked me up and we tore-ass to Stratford where we promptly got in line at the drive-thru of the Dixi-Kreme. We ordered the biggest cheeseburgers they had.

It felt great. Even better than we had hoped. Not since the Christmas mornings of our childhood had an event so thoroughly lived up to the hype. I remember sitting at the light at Stratford and Vest Mill Road, Dorsey just staring at his license, not even bothered by his goofy smile or the shadow behind his head that made it look like he had a mullet. None of that mattered, because my brother had his license. And I realized that the plastic card he held in his hands was about as close to tangible, physical freedom as anyone could get.

Dorsey's first car was a 1963½ Galaxie 500. It smoked a little, used way too much gas and rattled like a hardware store in an earthquake. But he loved it, and so did I. He had found it in an old tobacco barn, wasting away under a bunch of boxes and junk. I'd ridden out with Dorsey and Dad to look at the car. As my brother gazed down its knife-edged fenders and sleek curves with stars in his eyes, my father was crouching and peering into wheel wells, rapping his knuckles on quarter panels and kicking tires. He pulled Dorsey aside, outside the listing barn, out of earshot of the tiny, wrinkled woman who had answered the door.

"Son," he began gently. "I know this is what you've been looking for. I know you like it. But this car…"

We could all see it coming. I could tell Dad just didn't understand, the same way he didn't understand what made *Star Wars* every bit as good as *The Searchers*, or why "Detroit Rock City" excited us more than Merle Haggard. As Dad talked, Dorsey was peering back into the barn at the Galaxie. Even under the weight of all the junk and remains and years, she was gorgeous.

"This car is trouble, son. We don't even know if it runs." I could tell how hard Dad was trying not to break Dorsey's heart. "Who knows how much money it would take to get it drivable."

They were good points, all of them. But it didn't matter. Dorsey's mind had been made up the moment we'd driven up.

28

"I know, Dad," he said, and then for the next fifteen minutes he defended his intention of buying that car with the fervor and eloquence of a Founding Father espousing life and liberty. Finally my father sighed, clapped a strong hand over Dorsey's shoulder and nodded with a smile.

On our way home, Daddy's apprehension seemed to wisp out the open window along with the smoke from his cigarette until he finally flicked both away altogether.

"There's nothing friendly about a car like that," he began. "Those cars were built for one thing. Going fast." He tried to mask the enthusiasm in his voice. "They're brutal, unforgiving cars. All the refinement of a baseball bat." I could see him gripping the wheel a little tighter, the slightest smile creasing his lips. "As subtle as a sledge hammer." He drove a little faster. In my father's eyes I could see the ghosts of cars past. For miles he stared at the road's vanishing point as he talked to Dorsey about the car he'd just purchased as if he were warning him against marrying a dangerous woman he knew would break his heart. A woman he knew was no good. But a woman he knew his son was useless to resist. And he did know. He had answered that same siren's song, been smashed on those same rocks a generation earlier despite his own father's wishes. It had been Daddy's stories about his first car, a '51 Ford with a cackling flathead motor just like Robert Mitchum's from *Thunder Road*, that had given Dorsey and me the fever in the first place. And I realized that Dorsey wasn't being talked out of it so much as he was being prepared. For the good times and the bad. For better or worse.

29

"These cars are dangerous, son. Take her for granted, just once, and she can kill you. The power-to-weight ratio in a car like that…" He trailed off and then started again. "If you want to just gas and go, and never have to worry about setting your breaker points or adjusting the float level in your carburetor, this ain't the car for you. If you don't want to have to learn all that stuff, if you're scared to bust your knuckles, then let's turn around and go get your money back."

Dorsey assured our father that he was ready. He promised him that he could handle the responsibility. It was like listening to Luke Skywalker trying to convince Uncle Owen he was ready to join the Academy. Just like Owen, Dad was dubious.

"It's going to be loud," he said. "It'll make all your clothes smell like gasoline. It won't be comfortable. You'll sweat to death in the summer and freeze in the winter. It'll make your arms sore and your feet hot."

Dorsey couldn't stop smiling. Dad looked over at him and matched his grin.

We went to work right away. It didn't take us long to get it running. Running well, though, would be months away. The 390 initially refused to confine its combustion to the internal side. It leaked oil like a sieve and smoked like a freight train. Brand new, the big block put out 330 horsepower, but that was almost two decades and over 150,000 miles ago. On our first few trial runs, anything that could break, burn or burst did so with regularity.

On the late nights, Daddy would fire up the kerosene heater in the garage, put on a pot of coffee and turn on WTQR.

We'd listen to Don Williams and the Bellamy Brothers and Tom T. Hall as we worked. Sometimes we worked as team, ganging up a stubborn starter, Dad with a ratchet, Dorsey with the Vise-Grips and me with a crow bar. Other times we worked solo, one of us hunched over a dusty fender, another on his back under the transmission, the other doubled up under the dash. Endless hours we toiled, like a trio of mad scientists in a greasy lab. We replaced the heavy cast iron intake with a lightweight aluminum one. We scrapped the old, wheezing Autolite carburetors in favor of heavy-breathing Holleys. We discarded the constrictive exhaust manifolds for free-flowing headers. New battery, belts and hoses. Light bulbs and fuses. Anything we didn't replace got painted or polished.

Momma came out to check on us only once, snapping a photograph of the three of us kneeling by one of the Galaxie's gleaming chrome wheels. The wheel reflected distortions of my father and brother on either side, my mother holding the camera to her eye, the old garage all around, and in the center of it all, me, twisting and spiraling, surrounded by chrome and home. I gazed into that wheel like it was some kind of crystal ball. But I didn't see the future. All I saw was the present.

For the next three months, my brother, my dad and me practically lived in the garage. The guys at South Fork Auto Parts became good friends. After a couple of weeks I stopped trying to get my nails clean. Every shirt in my closet slowly turned 10W-40 black. Momma complained about the laundry. Grandma wondered how Dorsey would afford the insurance. His friends got tired of always having to drive. Never once did Dad say, "I told you so."

And when that garage door finally opened, and the windows shook and the neighbors peered through the blinds, instead of staggering out to the school bus bleary-eyed and half-alive, my brother drove to school in his own car.

"Promise me one thing," Daddy had said to Dorsey one night near the end. Dorsey nodded wordlessly. "Drive it," Dad intoned simply. "Don't baby it. I want you to be safe, obviously. Don't do anything stupid. But drive this car. Drive her within an inch of her life. Then we'll replace the things that break or fall off. Then drive her some more. It's what she's made for."

Dorsey promised. We had hit the Strip in it every weekend since.

Stratford Road was a 10-mile long stretch that ran from the stuffy, old money section of Buena Vista, south through the most commercialized, congested part of town. The Strip, the circuit used for cruising, consisted of the busiest two miles, the stretch where Dorsey and I had spent virtually every Friday and Saturday night all summer, cruising back and forth in his Galaxie. The turnaround on the north end was, depending on who you were cruising with, either the Thruway Shopping Center or the Five Points intersection just another half-mile up the road. On the southern end, the Strip terminated with the new Hanes Mall, its sprawling parking lot providing the obvious place to turn around and cruise north again. In between were service stations, the textile mill and the Dixi-Kreme, its sign staying lit well past midnight. The red neon pig dancing over licks of flame was a beacon illuminating the Strip. There were diners, ice cream parlors, the AMF lanes and about ten stoplights, all providing the perfect opportunity to rev up your engine at the guy in the lane beside you and see who could get to the next light the fastest. There was the jewelry place and its big clock tower, robbing anyone with a curfew of an excuse for coming home late; Rogers Chevrolet with rows of what passed for Corvettes and Camaros those days. On the east side, the train tracks ran parallel to the Strip for its entire length. At the north end of the Strip, Stratford crossed Interstate 40, and if you looked to the east you could see the three or four downtown buildings that were tall enough to rise above the tree line. Under the bridge, cars and trucks zoomed past, headed west to the mountains and east to the coast, while above, we just rode back and forth, going nowhere fast.

Dorsey and I had been cruising Stratford when he decided he wasn't going to college. He made sure of that when he decided not to take that second year of French his Senior year, which automatically disqualified him from acceptance in a state-system school. And since he only applied to state schools, he knew he'd get nothing but rejections. Which is exactly what he got.

We were standing in the lot of Parkway Ford when he made up his mind, he told me later. It was close to midnight, our last stop after cruising Stratford Road before meeting our curfew. It had just started to snow and the rows of shiny new Mustang GTs were slowly morphing from Bright Yellow, Midnight Blue Metallic and Bittersweet Glow to spring-flurry white. Across the lot, the half-finished addition to the showroom seemed to sprout from the asphalt, steel beams reaching up, connecting to others. And it had dawned on Dorsey, right then and there, that if he went off to school next fall he wouldn't get to see Parkway Ford's new showroom completed.

Granted, he had been contemplating it for months. I knew he didn't want to leave, but he felt like he was supposed to. That's what smart kids did and Dorsey considered himself a smart kid. Sure, he made mostly C's with the occasional B, but he took Honors classes. So he felt at least semi-smart. And even the semi-smart kids went off to college. The not-so-smart kids hung around town and went to work. But if you wanted to be an architect or astronomer of marine biologist, then you needed to go off to school. But Dorsey had no idea what he wanted to do with his life and Winston-Salem was as good a place as any to have no idea. He never told me any of that, but I knew.

So, that snowy spring night as I ogled new Mustangs and Dorsey contemplated new construction, he decided to take Auto Tech at Career Center instead of French as his final elective, not for a moment thinking of the not-so-smart kids who had grown up and had to get up in a few shorts hours in the dark and cold to get back to work on that half-built showroom. When the letters started coming back in the spring and Dorsey had to tell Dad that he didn't get in, and the old man tried to mask his disappointment that yet another generation wouldn't be going to college, Dorsey pleaded ignorance to the two foreign language policy the state had implemented a couple of years earlier. He said he was robbed. He said he was smart enough; he had the grades (barely), but simply didn't have the right combination of credits. He was a victim of red tape. A casualty of bureaucracy. Had he only known about the new requirements...

Dad didn't buy it, of course. Not for a minute. He knew Dorsey didn't want to go and I think he sympathized. But he would've liked it better had Dorsey just come right out and said he didn't want to go and told him why. He would have understood. He would have felt the same way. But Dorsey also didn't want to disappoint him, so he had to at least try. Or rather, present the illusion of trying. Because maybe Dad would be less disappointed that way. And I think Dad even understood all of that. So he pretended not to be disappointed in any of it. And maybe he really wasn't.

Arnold Rayburn, our neighbor a few houses up, owned Cloverdale Shell and offered Dorsey a job when Arnold Jr. went off to college. Dorsey started out as an attendant, sauntering out to the full-service island like Pavlov's dog whenever he'd hear the *ding-ding...ding-ding* to fill'er up and wash off a windshield with that awesome squeegee and a pale blue paper towel, maybe check the oil while he was at it and, if they had kids, bring out a handful of Super Bubble when he brought the receipt. Eventually Arnold gave Dorsey a promotion of sorts and let him rotate a few tires and replace the occasional fan belt, which was child's play for Dorsey, who was born to turn wrenches. Arnold realized this soon enough, and it wasn't long until Dorsey was made a full-time mechanic at the station and given a set of keys, which meant

35

Dorsey had to close up by himself every other Saturday afternoon. Which, in turn, meant that I spent a lot of time hanging out at Cloverdale Shell waiting on Dorsey to get off work so we could go cruising.

I loved hanging out at the station with Dorsey. I loved sitting on that rickety wooden stool in the office and flipping through car parts catalogs and eating Slim Jims and drinking Cokes in the little glass bottles. I loved going out to the bays while Dorsey maybe did a brake job or flushed a radiator. That smell of gasoline and grease and tires. The hundreds of belts and hoses that hung from a clothes line strung from one painted block wall to the other, most covered with a fine powder of dust, but every now and then there'd be a shiny black new one Arnold had ordered to replace one Dorsey had used on a customer's car. I loved pestering Dorsey until he finally gave in and ran me up and down on the lift. More than anything I think I loved having a brother who was a mechanic at a service station. It made me feel like some kind of an insider.

On this particular Saturday afternoon Dorsey had a little old lady who needed a last minute inspection on her 1967 Dodge Coronet, which put him half an hour late locking the doors. It was already starting to get dark when we emerged at the south end of the Strip, waiting for our light to turn. To our right Stratford Road yawned off into the dusk, the street lights ending, four lanes shrinking to two. To our left, everything.

We sat at the light, poking our nose out to see better, our left turn signal blinking patiently. The western sky was a finger

36

paint smear of pink and mauve. The sun was dropping quickly behind the trees, and casting mottled shadows and orange patches of light. At this time of day, right before sunset, the Galaxie's paint always looked its best. The red seemed a little deeper and the swirls and scratches weren't as visible. The uneven gaps in the panels were masked by shadows and the waves in the sheet metal seemed to disappear. Sunset made the old girl look ten years younger.

Down the Strip we could see the traffic, lined up in both directions, red taillights on the right, white headlights on the left, like a pair of ruby and diamond necklaces laid side-by-side. We got the green and pulled out, quickly catching up to the tail end of the line and slowing to a stop. I peered ahead; bumper-to-bumper as far as the eye could see, inching forward, elbows hanging out every window. Drifting on the evening breeze was a symphony of overlapping rock n' roll songs mingling with idling V8s, punctuated every few seconds by a honking horn, a girl's bubbling laughter or a squealing tire in the distance. We had grown up listening to our dad's stories about the cars they'd driven, the girls that rode with them, the races they'd won and lost. We'd grown up building Monogram and Revell kits of 440 Six-Packs and Super Sport Malibu's and Cobra Jet Mustangs. Now we were the ones prowling the Strip in our own cars, turning Stratford Road into an asphalt catwalk every weekend.

This was going to be our last time doing this, though. I knew it even if Dorsey didn't. Last spring I had been accepted to N.C. State. The campus was less than two hours down I-40, but it was a world away. I was leaving Monday morning. College kids didn't cruise Stratford, I knew, and after this weekend I was going to be a college kid. Even if Stratford Road was still going to be there for me, I wouldn't be there for it.

"Crowded tonight," I pointed out.

"Yeah. Lots of kids these days," Dorsey said. He reached into the floorboard behind my seat and flipped open his alligator skin 8-track case. From its red velvet slot, he selected KISS's *Alive II* and jammed it into the player. The sound of a rabid crowd rose in the car, like a swelling sea. I closed my eyes and imagined the scene at the Los Angeles Forum. The opening act had finished, the roadies had done their feverish, stooped dance and the waiting was over. The arena had gone dark and the crowd erupted. A snarling voice from somewhere, the bowels of backstage maybe, was maniacally preaching to the sweaty, impatient throng. "You wanted the best, you got the best!"

The driving opening licks of "Detroit Rock City" built like an erupting volcano. As Paul Stanley wailed, Gene's bass line slinked around the drumbeat like a charmed cobra. I pictured the stage slowly disappearing behind a creeping bank of dry ice fog, the vapor seeming to pulse and glow internally whenever the bright white lights from the KISS sign flashed and strobed. From monolithic walls of amps a perfect storm of sound blasted forth; a maelstrom of swirling, grinding guitars, throbbing bass and pummeling drums.

This was a ritual, I realized. A ceremony. The crowd raised its incantation to the rafters. The band were shamans;

intermediaries between the human and divine. They were there simply to pave the way, to help me commune with the spirit of rock 'n' roll. Their job was to open the portal to this strange new realm, and to prepare my mind and soul to shout it out loud. It was a kind of magic.

The KISS show, in some very real ways, was also a battle. Gene, Paul, Peter and Ace were the field generals, and the enthralled masses pumping their fists in the air were the foot soldiers, struggling against forces real and perceived. Parents, teachers, preachers, bosses, peers, girls, hormones, responsibility, adolescence, encroaching adulthood. Forces eternally aligned against the KISS fan, if only for these few teenaged years. Yet forces whose conquering seemed so perpetually crucial that it got continually updated, retooled and restaged for each new generation. Even at that age, I understood that KISS had maybe five years left to fight that battle, if they were lucky.

We made one circuit of the Strip before Dorsey blurted out, "I'm hungry."

The line at the drive-thru at the Dixi-Kreme was wrapped all the way around the building. The place had only sported a drive-thru for about a year and was the first restaurant in town to have one. The delay in adding a drive-thru was because there was no good way to route traffic through it. The building was constructed well before I was born, which meant it pre-dated drive-thru's by a couple of decades. When they drew up the plans, the idea of getting your cheeseburger passed to you from a window probably didn't even cross their minds. The side of the building that would have otherwise had the drive-thru window was backed up against Stratford Road so tightly that a driveway wouldn't fit. They were able to put the menu board and speaker on the driver's side but had no choice but to ask customers to drive up with the restaurant itself on the passenger's side of their cars. This of course meant that if you were by yourself you had to lean across your front seat and crank your window down, then reach further still to hand your money to the surly teenager in the red-checkered uniform, then reach again to grab your sack of greasy food. This was a nearly impossible feat if you were in a 1963½ Galaxie, for example. In that particular situation, one might have to put the car in neutral, set the parking brake (and hope it held) then slide into the passenger's seat to put oneself within arm's reach of your footlong all-the-way.

This was all much easier if you had a co-pilot, naturally, and since I was with Dorsey he wouldn't need a chiropractor after this particular visit to the Dixi-Kreme. The line moved at a snail's pace but we finally made it to the speaker and were ready for our turn to order. Dorsey pulled up until his window was next to the illuminated menu board.

"Well, Deney Terrio," a squawking, crackling parrot said to us from the perforated circle at the bottom of the menu board. "Rayon fake disorder, tease?"

Without hesitation Dorsey placed our order. "Yeah, give me two Dubble Delux combos, one with a Cheerwine, one with a Dr. Pepper."

A lengthy pause followed, then the parrot said, "Rats do trouble a ducks riff a fear rind and a rocker pecker?"

"Yep," came Dorsey's confident reply.

Then the insane parrot said, "Jew on a jump old flies brat?"

Finally Dorsey seemed stumped. "Excuse me?" he said politely.

The parrot barked at him, "Huge song of thump oh sight fat?"

Dorsey looked at me, sheer confusion in his expression.

"I think they want to know if we want to jumbo-size it," I offered.

Dorsey nodded at me and then turned to address the menu board once more. "No thanks."

Then the parrot seemed to gargle and spit in the microphone, then said something that sounded vaguely like, "Peas fly aloud."

Dorsey was now visibly agitated. "Please drive around," he spat. "Yeah, okay. Considering the fact that this line hasn't moved in ten minutes, we'll drive around. Yeah, we'll be right there. Here we come."

I couldn't help but chuckle a little, even though I knew it would only make it worse.

Dorsey continued. "And if I wanted to jumbo size it, I would have said, 'Jumbo size that shit, bitch'. Jesus. I hate that."

"How do you really feel about it?" I said, openly laughing now, adding fuel to Dorsey's fire.

"I got your jumbo size right here!" Dorsey said to the menu board. Now he was laughing, too. "I got your jumbo size swinging, you damn Mack Donald's wannabe. You damn parrot-sounding bitch. With your stupid-ass drive-thru and your busted-ass speaker. Why don't you please drive around on my jumbo-sized pecker!"

Suddenly the menu board speaker crackled to life again. "I hope you know I can hear everything you're saying," came the voice, only this time it was crystal clear.

Dorsey's eye flew wide as saucers. He looked at me, silently pleading for help of some kind, any kind. All I could do was wipe the tears from my eyes as I held my aching side. He spun in his seat and looked behind us, assessing the viability of a reverse getaway. No dice. We were closed in, at least half a dozen cars stacked up behind us.

"Shit," he whispered. His face was ghost-white.

"Don't worry about it," I coughed through my laughter. "She won't be at the window."

Dorsey didn't utter another word until we pulled up to the window after about ten more minutes of waiting in line. Inside stood a pleasant-looking girl, maybe 16-years old, braces and freckles. She smiled sweetly at us and chirped, "That'll be $5.17."

Dorsey finally exhaled, his thoughts no doubt mirroring my own; no way this was the girl who took our order, she's being way too friendly.

My brother handed me a fist full of crumpled bills and I added a few of my own, then handed the whole mess to the nice

42

girl. In return she handed me a crisp white bag full of burgers and fries, then passed our drinks to me along with our change.

"Thanks," I said.

"Thank you," the Dixi-Kreme girl said happily. As we began to pull away, she ducked to see across the car to Dorsey and said, "Have fun driving around with your jumbo-sized pecker."

Dorsey looked like he was going to throw up. I was laughing so hard I thought I might, too.

It was almost dark by the time we got back out on the Strip. Dorsey flipped on the dome light so I could check our food for loogies and boogers and pubic hair, because surely there was some combination of the three tucked neatly under a pickle after the stunt he just pulled.   I was still wiping the tears from my eyes when I looked over at my big brother and tried like hell to not think about the fact that I wouldn't be here next weekend. Or the weekend after that. I tried not to concentrate on that part of me that knew I'd really never be here and now again.

The sky had turned a deep, inky blue and underneath it the Strip was ablaze with light; the reds, yellows and greens of the stoplights, scarlet neon on roadside business signs, the greenish-blue of the staggered streetlights, crimson taillights, white headlights, blinking amber turn signals, and off in the distance the pulsing, syncopated blue on the roof of a police cruiser. Dorsey piloted the Galaxie through the lightshow, the colors slip-sliding across the hood like rainbow-colored comets, the Rangoon red shifting across the spectrum - violet, magenta, vermilion - depending on the reflections in the paint.

I finished examining our burgers and approved them for human consumption, and we dug in. Between stuffing French fries in his mouth, Dorsey reached into his tape case and replaced *Alive II* with *Candy-O* by The Cars.

Dorsey and I belted out "Let's Go", operatically attesting to how much we liked the nightlife, baby. For weeks after Dorsey first bought *Candy-O* I would steal it from his car and hide away in my bedroom for hours, sitting on my carpet with my headphones on, staring at the Alberto Vargas cover art: a strawberry blonde pin-up in a smoke-colored body stocking lounging on the sleek hood of a Ferrari 365 GTC/4. It took multiple consultations with Dad's old girlie mags and Dorsey's car mags to deduce the respective identities of the artist and the automobile, but I was dedicated. (It should be noted here that at the time I cared more about the Ferrari, and the line drawing of it, than the scantily-clad lass on said Ferrari's hood. That would soon change.)

"Greatest album cover of all-time," I said.

Dorsey regarded it momentarily then gave a slow shake of his head.

"I don't know, man." Dorsey perused his selection of 8-tracks until he produced Molly Hatchet's self-titled debut. On the tape's weathered sticker, upon a massive onyx steed was the Death Dealer, his hulking, armored frame barely concealed by a scarred metal shield. In his hand he clutched a battle axe, blood

44

dripping from its talon-like point. Beneath his horned and spiked helm, his eyes burned a hellish red. "Pretty badass, huh?"

"Not as badass as this," I said, and pulled out *Bat Out of Hell* by Meat Loaf. On the cover, a motorcycle burst from a fissure in the earth, its driver hauling back on the handlebars as if breaking a wild stallion, every muscle on his body standing out angrily as he straddled the bike's tangle of chromium steel pipes.

"That might be badass," Dorsey said, pulling a different tape from the case, "But this is a nice ass." He showed me Whitesnake's *Lovehunter*: a giant horned serpent and its naked rider, her back arched, head thrown back, apparently in the throes of orgasm astride the beast's scaly back.

I countered with .38 Special's *Wild-Eyed Southern Boys* and its airbrushed depiction of the boys in the band ogling a sweet young thang in pink satin hot pants. "Nicer ass," I proclaimed.

"I'll show you a nice ass," Dorsey said, scanning the tape case. "Hang on." He looked back at me with a triumphant smirk on his face. "Can't believe I didn't think of this one right off the bat," he said, almost to himself, as he slowly unveiled his selection.

It was an ass, alright. An ass that filled the entire cover, clad in skintight tomato-red leather, and a hairy hand with a pair of crossed fingers draped across it.

"Dude," I began my measured response. "That's a dude's ass."

Dorsey snapped the tape around to make sure he had the right one.

45

"Bullshit," he said after confirming that he was, in fact, holding Loverboy's *Get Lucky*.

"Look at the hand," I said. "You ever seen a chick with a forearm that hairy?"

"Well, sure, the hand is a guy's," Dorsey said. "But he's got his arm around the girl in the leather pants."

"It's his right hand. And it's coming from the right side. Right?"

Dorsey examined the image, but conceded nothing.

"So, unless your imagined lover boy is standing in front of this alleged woman with his back to her—"

"Okay, okay," Dorsey interjected, hoping I'd drop it.

"You've been checking out Mike Reno's ass."

"Fuck you."

"How many times have you beat off to it?"

"Seriously, fuck you." Dorsey stuffed the tape back into its slot and turned his attention to his rear view mirror.

"No, really, it's okay, man," I went on. "I'm not judging you. If that's what you're into..." Dorsey wasn't listening anymore. I figured he was simply tuning me out but I hadn't noticed the headlights looming behind us.

"Dude's riding our ass awful close," he said after a long drag off his Cheerwine.

I checked my side mirror. There, just inches off our back bumper, was a Mustang. I couldn't tell what year. I turned and craned my neck to see. "What is it?"

"Don't be so obvious," Dorsey said. "We don't want him to know we know, you know?"

"Okay, okay. " I turned back around. "But what is it?"

"Boss 429. NASCAR engine. Back in '69, Ford claimed they made only 375 horsepower, but that was just to fool the insurance companies. The truth was well over 400. Baddest Mustang ever made. Hell, maybe the baddest muscle car ever made."

"Shit," I whispered.

"Yeah."

In his rearview mirror Dorsey kept a close eye on the Mustang. He was two feet off our bumper at most. Dorsey handed his half-finished Dubble Delux to me.

"Here," he said. "Hold this."

"What about your drink?"

"Nah, it's fine." He took a long draw from his straw and then tucked his Cheerwine back between his legs.

He gripped the shifter and hovered his left foot over the clutch pedal.

"Grab hold of something," he said.

I latched onto the armrest with one hand and cradled my fries and drink in my lap with the other.

I could hear the Mustang's engine begin to whine before he actually made his move. He whipped his steering wheel and dove into the adjacent lane, the front of his car lifting as he gunned it.

Dorsey jammed the shifter into second gear, tached up the 390 and then dropped the clutch. The tires let out a screech before

47

getting traction and we began to furiously accelerate. I was scrambling to keep the food in my lap, but when Dorsey shifted again and we launched forward with another burst speed, my Dr. Pepper tumbled into the floor at my feet, flooding the rubber mat with cola.

The road ahead was free of cars till well past the next light. If we could just hold him off, I thought, hold him off until we had to brake for the next stoplight, then Dorsey could say he'd raced a Boss 429 and didn't lose.

No sooner had I formulated that idea in my head than a deafening, feral roar filled my ears and the Mustang rocketed past like we were sitting still, distinctive *III*-shaped taillights diminishing rapidly. He slipped under the next stoplight but the one after that caught him. There was no one in the lane next to him.

Dorsey would never admit it, but I could tell he was lying back, hoping the light would turn green before we got there in time for the rematch. He slowed, coasting toward the red light, tapping the brakes. The light wasn't changing. We could hear the sound of the big 429 idling lazily as we neared. Still the light stayed red. Finally we pulled alongside the Boss and crept to a halt, door to door. Even sitting still that car looked like it was going a hundred miles an hour; the chin spoiler, so low it looked like it might scrape the asphalt; the angled, shark-like nose; that long, sleek hood, a gaping maw of a scoop perched on top. It looked positively predatory.

After a few awkward, silent moments of sitting and staring at the stoplight, Dorsey and I slowly turned our heads in unison to steal a glance at the Mustang's driver. I don't know what I expected. Steve McQueen, maybe. Paul Newman. Ace Frehley. But it was just a guy. A regular, normal-looking guy. He was older than us, in his early 30's I'd say. By himself. Gently tapping his fingers on his steering wheel to a song we couldn't hear.

He seemed to realize suddenly he was being watched and looked our way, giving a barely perceptible nod. Dorsey and I snapped our heads back straight and forward, not saying a word.

That damned red light seemed frozen. Dorsey instinctively checked the rearview, for what I wasn't sure. Cops, maybe. But no, that would mean he was thinking of racing this guy again. Then he slowly pushed the accelerator to the floor, the Galaxie's engine snarling, flexing its muscles.

The look on my face asked the question for me.

"I know what I'm doing," Dorsey said, his voice low and calm.

Then a sound came from the Mustang, a sound like a demon's roar. It was as if a lion had just roared back at hissing housecat. I could see the back end of his car lifting, but the car itself made no forward progress. I knew what he was doing. He had the Mustang in gear, one foot on the brake pedal locking the car in place, and the other foot on the gas, easing into it until he found that sweet spot where the back tires would spin but the front brakes would keep the car from moving. Drag racers called it a line-lock.

The sound of his engine steadily grew louder, the back end of the car canting upward as the back tires began to scrape at the pavement, barely beginning to turn. They twitched and shifted until suddenly they lost traction and started spinning freely. Faster and faster they spun, the car not budging. A steady plume of white smoke began to float away from the tires, in wispy tendrils at first then in rolling clouds until the entire storefront was enshrouded by it. Within seconds, the intersection was flooded with the smell of burning rubber and the choking smoke that accompanied it. I plugged my ears against the shrieking tires and roaring engine, then decided the smell was worse than the noise and moved my hands to cover my nose. Dorsey turned and said something to me but I couldn't hear a word of it.

Through a break in the smoke, I could see the driver of the Mustang behind the wheel, a smug grin curling his mouth. He kept it going for another few seconds, letting out his brake ever so slowly, the frantic spinning of the tires finally pushing the car forward. Our light turned green and the Mustang shot out from the cloud. With the howl of the engine still echoing all around us, he was gone.

"That son of a bitch," Dorsey spat.

"Let it go, man. So what if he's got a faster car than you?"

"He doesn't."

Dorsey gunned it and blasted down to the next red light where the Mustang was sitting, waiting again. No sooner had we come to a complete halt than the light flashed green. The Boss and Dorsey floored it at the exact same moment. I was thrown back in his seat like I had been kicked in the chest by a mule. Our tires were spinning, seeking purchase. I could hear the Mustang's doing likewise, and the RPMs of both cars suddenly climbed as we shot from the gates at the same time. The rich smell of spent gasoline filled my nostrils while the sounds of our engines being unleashed rattled my skull.

I squeezed my eyes shut and prayed for it to be over with. Even over the scream of Dorsey's engine I could hear the roar of the 429. It sounded like it was going to crawl through my window at any moment. I tried again to sit up but the force of our acceleration kept me pinned. I could hear the Boss shift into second gear, accompanied by the yelp of his tires breaking loose again. The sound of his engine seemed to shift in proximity, like maybe he was fading back. Like maybe Dorsey was pulling away.

A few seconds later, we shifted into second, and still the Mustang seemed to fall back. Still we accelerated, gathering speed like a rocket trying to escape Earth's gravity. The sound of Dorsey's engine was deafening. I could no longer hear the 429.

And just like that, the roar of Dorsey's motor became a whisper, the forward momentum ceased with such suddenness it catapulted me upright. It was over. One way or the other, it was over. I opened my eyes and looked over my shoulder, scanning the street behind us for the Mustang, wondering how badly Dorsey had beaten him. There was no sign of him.

"Shit," I gasped. "Where is he?"

Dorsey raised his hand and pointed up ahead. I looked and saw nothing at first. But there, about two blocks away, I could

51

make out a pair of vertical taillights. They brightened just as I saw them, the driver finally getting on the brakes.

"Oh." I slumped back into my seat. Dorsey could only nod.

The next light caught us and we stopped and just sat there. I looked at my brother. I didn't know what to say. His eyes indicated a vow was being made, solemnly, that this would never happen again. Even if it meant pouring every paycheck he earned for the next ten years into this car, Dorsey would never lose another race on Stratford Road. The image of the Boss' driver flashed in his head at that moment, and just as quickly it was replaced by Dorsey, a decade from now, in his early 30's, still doing the exact same thing he was doing right now.

"You've got the green, dude," I said after letting Dorsey sit, oblivious, for a few seconds after our light had changed. He snapped out of it and we slowly moved away.

For a few circuits Dorsey seemed to be on autopilot, driving like a zombie, simply going through the motions. All around us zipped tiny hatchbacks and compacts, driven by kids who didn't look old enough to have their licenses. The Galaxie suddenly felt old and massive, like an aged ocean liner lumbering amongst swift runabouts. We rolled to a stop under a yellow light Dorsey could've easily ran. We sat wordlessly and listened to the engine idle.

A sound like a shot from a rifle made both of us jump out of our seats. Smack in the center of Dorsey's windshield was a burst raw egg, the shrapnel of the shell scattered across the glass, the slimy white and yellow insides sliding down to the wipers.

52

"God," Dorsey started slowly. Then, "Dammit! Who the hell was that?" Dorsey barked. "Who did that?"

I leaned out the window to get a make and model of the drive-by egger. "Trans Am," I reported. "Black. New one."

I could see Dorsey's grip on the steering wheel tighten and his eyes darken. "Amber," he hissed.

The Amber that Dorsey so venomously referred to was Amber Myers, his ex-girlfriend and former West Forsyth Titans cheerleader, Class of '77. The break-up was ugly, with Amber accusing Dorsey (wrongly) of making out with Sylvia Adkins at the Aerosmith concert, and Dorsey accusing Amber (rightly) of doing a striptease to KC and the Sunshine Band's "That's the Way (I Like It)" for the entire football team in the locker room after West beat Reynolds.

With a burst of movement, Dorsey threw the Galaxie into first gear and cranked the wheel around, and we bolted down the nearest side street. Amber's Trans Am slipped into the darkness in the other direction.

"Were not going after them?" I demanded.

"Not like this we're not," Dorsey replied, an eerie calm in his voice. "We've got to get cleaned up. Then we'll need ammo."

Dorsey, peering through smears of egg-white, guided the Galaxie into the nearest parking lot. He hopped out and rounded the rear of the car, opening the trunk and returning quickly with a rag and shoebox-sized brown paper sack he tossed through the window into my lap. Within seconds, Dorsey had the windshield more or less translucent again and us underway.

53

"Go ahead," he said, nodding to the package. "Check it out."

I opened up the sack and pulled out a cellophane-wrapped brick of bottle rockets. In the spaces on the label between the Chinese characters were desperate warnings about keeping fireworks away from children and where not to shoot them and who not to shoot them at. I was cautioned about explosives and flammables and loud noises and eyes and ears and fingers. I was suddenly overcome with a feeling that Dorsey intended to blatantly ignore every warning the Chinese could throw at him. The label also said there were one hundred bottle rockets inside and that they would soar over 200 feet into the sky before exploding into a rainbow-colored shower of sparks. I remembered these rockets. Dorsey had bought them along with about $50 worth of Black Cats, ladyfingers, M-80s and Roman candles at a giant fireworks outlet just outside Myrtle Beach two summers ago.

"What, exactly, are we going to do with these?" I asked.

"Air-to-air missiles," came Dorsey's calm response.

"Missiles."

"Yep." Dorsey's eyes were glued to the road.

I didn't ask any more questions.

The crowd on the strip had thinned a little, the kids with midnight curfews on their way home. We fell into line in front of Putt-Putt and I immediately began scanning the opposing lanes, looking for the tell-tale "screaming chicken" decal on the hood of

Amber's Trans Am. We made two circuits of the Strip before we saw what we were looking for.

"There," I pointed. It was a T/A, alright.

"Nope." Dorsey gave a dismissive shake of his head. As the Pontiac drew closer we could see its paintjob was charcoal gray, not Amber's black. "Get ready just in case," he said. I unwrapped the bottle rockets, stuffing the cellophane back in to the sack and tucking the sack under my seat. I reached over and pushed in the cigarette lighter in Dorsey's dash.

We went on radio silence, Dorsey turning off *Candy-O* in midstream. After a minute the lighter popped back out, ready. Both of us watched the street ahead and the side roads and parking lots, looking for any sign of our quarry.

Without warning, Dorsey spun the steering wheel, whipping the car around and making a U-turn in the middle of Stratford Road. One car had to swerve to miss us and three more had to lock down their brakes. Dorsey orchestrated a frantic three-point turn to avoid jumping the curb, and then we were back in traffic heading the other way.

"Where?" I asked with steely reserve.

"Five cars up," Dorsey said.

I don't know how we missed her. Dorsey waited for gaps in traffic and shot ahead, one position at a time until Amber's Tran Am was only one car away in the right lane, us in the left.

I pushed the cigarette lighter in again. I could see Amber behind the wheel, another girl sitting in the passenger seat and another pair in the back. All four were seemingly talking at the

55

same time, hands gesturing about, heads tossed around in laughter. The lighter popped back out and I looked at Dorsey. He gave me a solemn nod. I pulled the lighter out and checked it, confirming the glowing orange spiral inside. I plucked a bottle rocket from the batch and held the lighter against the fuse.

The fuse began spewing putrid smoke and I quickly held the thing out the window. Dorsey took the lighter from my hand and I propped myself up on the seat, angling my body outside. I held my arm straight out away from me, tilting my head away, closing one eye and doing my best to aim the rocket at Amber's open window. The fuse burned down to nothing and then a plume of white smoke shot from the tiny barrel on the end of the stick. As soon I felt it tugging away, I let go.

We watched as the rocket shot away, spiraling slowly as it flew toward Amber's car. For a moment it looked as if it would score a direct hit, like it was heading straight at Amber's left ear. But at the last second, the rocket rolled and arced upward with a whistling screech, streaming maybe 50 yards into the dark sky before issuing a sharp *POP!* and spitting a few white sparks that barely qualified as a trickle, much less the advertised shower. No matter. We weren't concerned with a light show. Our mission was to terrorize.

Before I realized it, Dorsey was handing me another bottle rocket, the fuse already burning. He had maneuvered us closer still, Amber's Trans Am just off our front corner now. I pointed the rocket at the car, holding it by the stick until it began to pull and then I let it fly. This one instantly shot skyward, soaring high

56

above the Holiday Inn across the railroad tracks, whistling for a few seconds before popping with a flash.

Dorsey handed me the cigarette lighter and I stabbed in into its socket in the dash.

"Hurry, hurry," Dorsey said, one eye on traffic, the other on his ex-girlfriend. We had almost pulled even with her. I glanced at the girls. They were still perfectly oblivious, unaware of our presence, much less our aerial attacks.

I snatched the lighter away as soon as it popped up and I lit another fuse. This time I hung my whole upper body out the window of the car, stretching out my arm and aiming the rocket directly at Amber's head. We were so close now I could have thrown the firecracker into their window. Suddenly the bottle rocket began to shoot its smoke and I released it. Immediately it dove downward, skipping across the asphalt and disappearing under Amber's car. There was a pregnant pause, Dorsey and me waiting, then from beneath Amber's car came an ear-splitting shriek and then a flash of light and a *POW!* like a gunshot.

Amber and her friends were oblivious no longer. In unison the four of them began to scream, hands flailing as they frantically looked all about them for the source of the noise. Dorsey and I exploded in laughter, exchanging high fives between pointing at Amber and holding our sides. The stoplight ahead turned yellow, then red, and we came to a stop, still a car-length behind Amber. I could see her looking this way and that, trying to figure out what had happened. Suddenly she looked back, her eyes landing on first me and then her ex-boyfriend.

Amber seemed to be climbing out of her window. She raised a pair of clenched fists and then extended both middle fingers. "Fuck you, Dorsey Bennett!" she barked. "You son of a bitch!" I was doubled over in my seat, laughing so hard I had begun to cough uncontrollably.

"Uh, dude," I heard Dorsey say. I could barely hear him over my laughter. "Dude," he said again, this time tugging on my sleeve. I looked at him, wiping the tears from my face. My brother's eyes were wide and he was repeatedly pointing at my lap. I followed the line of his finger until I saw the cigarette lighter in my hand, lying against the fuse of a bottle rocket.

I leapt from my seat, sending the rockets in every direction. Some landed on the dash, quite a few went in the floor and even more landed right back in my lap. Somewhere, among the pick-up sticks of bottle rockets strewn throughout the interior of Dorsey's car, was a live one. Desperately I shuffled through them, looking for smoke, watching for the glow of a lit fuse. Suddenly the car began to fill with an ashy cloud, and then a deafening whistle.

"Shit!" Dorsey shouted. We weren't laughing anymore. "Shit! Shit! Shit!"

And then from somewhere in the floorboard between my feet: *POW!* I waited for any signs of pain, like maybe a toe had been blown off. But no. I was unscathed. Dorsey and I exchanged nervous glances, then slowly began to chuckle.

Then Dorsey began to tug on my sleeve again. "Dude." His eyes were fixed on the lattice-work of bottle rockets in my lap. I looked down in time to see a plume of white smoke rising from my crotch.

A string of *dammit*'s spewed from me as I brushed the bottle rockets into the floor in a frenzy, scrambling up the seat-back in a futile effort to get away. The whole car was filling with a suffocating cloud of smoke. And then came the shrieks, dozens of them, one after the other, like bombs raining down. Then a sound rang out, not unlike a machine gun. No, an *army* of machine guns. Streams of sparks shot throughout the car in purple, cyan and green.

POW! POW! POW! POW!

I was curled up in my seat now, my feet tucked under my body, hands cupped over my ears, eyes clenched tight. I had no way of knowing how long it lasted. It couldn't have been more than a few seconds, because when I finally opened my eyes, our light was still red. As the last of the rocket's red glare faded away and the shrieks were silenced, I could hear the sound of four girls laughing riotously next to us. I looked over and saw Amber and her friends, their eyes welling up with tears, cheeks flushed as they pointed at us.

"Dorsey, you dipshit!" Amber gasped between laughs. "What a moron!"

I suddenly felt terrible. This was all my fault. I had ruined Dorsey's ultimate revenge. Not to mention his carpet, which was pockmarked now with smoking scorches.

Amber went on. "You're a big man, ain't you?" Our light finally turned green, and Amber mercifully began to pull away, but not before yelling out, "Maybe if you'd been a big man for real, I wouldn't have screwed the football team!"

And for the second time in an hour, I didn't know what to say to my brother.

Dorsey jammed the shifter into first gear and stomped the gas. The Galaxie's big motor bucked and we roared through the intersection, chasing after Amber and her friends. The light ahead turned yellow just as her Trans Am slip ped under. Dorsey had every intention of running the red. No way was he letting Amber get away.

"Cop," I said, matter-of-factly.

"Huh?"

"Cop."

"Shit."

The cop had just pulled up to the light not forty yards away, sitting perpendicular to the Strip. Dorsey frantically downshifted and stood on the brake pedal, the rear wheels locking up, screeching and hopping across the pavement, contrails of blue smoke swirling in our wake. Twenty yards away our light turned red. Our car was drifting sideways now, the back end moving across the yellow line into oncoming traffic. Ten yards. I could see the cop, looking the other way. The nose of the Galaxie dove toward the pavement, 3,700 pounds of steel and glass careening like a space capsule burning up on reentry. The cop's light turned green and he crept into the intersection, unaware of the skidding car heading straight for him. Ten feet now. Dorsey pulled the wheel to the right, pointing the car onto the grassy shoulder. We

60

were almost stopped but we weren't going to make it. At five feet, the cop made his turn and drove off. And we stopped.

Our engine had sputtered out during the slow-down and now we sat in the middle of Stratford Road, dead in the water and encircled by tire smoke. The cop was gone. He hadn't even looked our way.

"Nice one, bro," I said, gathering the bottle rockets from between my legs.

Then Dorsey said, slowly and quietly, "Dammit."

He was staring through the windshield. I looked to where his eyes were fixed and saw our cop, making a U-turn around a smattering of cars, the blue lights on his roof strobing.

As calmly as I could, I said simply, "Go."

Dorsey keyed the starter and, as if it were scripted, the engine spun uselessly but never fired off. He tried again, and once more the motor cranked and cranked but wouldn't catch. I watched the cop, weaving through traffic, making his way toward us. "Go," I said again.

"I'm trying," Dorsey seethed, hitting the starter again. The cop was still on the other side of the intersection, trying to find a clear route through the stopped cars. Drivers were trying to get out of his way but only making it worse, blocking his initial path and forcing him to reverse and redirect himself, buying us precious time.

Dorsey closed his eyes and rested his head against the steering wheel. "Come on, baby," he whispered. He turned the switch again and this time the 390 coughed once, then began to stutter and gurgle. He kept the key turned, the engine spinning, sputtering still, but beginning to fire. Then, with a booming backfire that echoed all the way down Stratford Road, the engine awoke with a roar.

Instantly Dorsey popped the clutch, tires spitting silt and rubble in a rooster tail behind us as we shot forward. We bounced onto the pavement, veering wildly before righting ourselves, then launching through the intersection. I scrambled to brace myself just as Dorsey hit the brakes hard and dove right. He yanked the shifter back and mashed the gas pedal to the floor, feeding fuel to the starved engine and sending us rocketing away.

Vest Mill Road opened up before us. In the mirror I could see the flashing blue lights and bouncing headlights of the cop car. He was cutting across the parking lot of Putt-Putt on a course to intercept, his only hope of catching us. I could see the white and blue Crown Victoria mowing down a row of orange traffic cones, sailing across swells and ridges in the pavement, and bounding over speed bumps, the beams of the headlights shooting all around; down at the asphalt below and then into the night sky like searchlights.

"Go, go, go," I chanted. The cop was pulling a lead on us, closing fast. Dorsey pushed the accelerator into the carpet, trying to push it right through the floor. The Galaxie clawed at the pavement, digging for speed. The police car streaked across the horizon beside us. He had the angle. If he kept his speed, he would emerge onto Vest Mill Road directly in front of us, blocking our escape route.

62

Then, as if a giant blanket had been dropped on it, the cop car simply disappeared. As we blasted by the point where our paths would have crossed, I looked out Dorsey's window just in time to see the police car launching out the drainage ditch it had dropped into and catapulting across the road in a lazy arc. In the red glow of our taillights I saw it dive nose-first into the pavement, the hood and fenders buckling. The car did a double-axel, plastic pieces flying off its shattered grill, almost somersaulting before dropping back on all fours and slaloming across the road to come to a rest in the opposite ditch.

I spun in my seat to survey the damage. The impact had completely disabled the car and it rested at the bottom of the ditch like a burnt-out meteor in a crater. Dorsey let out a whoop as he witnessed the defeated cop for himself in his mirror, gingerly extracting himself from the wreckage, shouting obscenities at us as we sped away.

We zigged and zagged through the backstreets for the next half-hour before Dorsey finally calmed down enough to loop back to Cloverdale Shell. We rolled to a stop in the darkened parking lot. I-40 arched overhead, constantly giving off a *clackity-clack* sound as tractor-trailers barreled across its expansion joints. Behind the station, Baptist Hospital rose like some kind of brick mutant.

Dorsey came around to my side of the Galaxie, where I was inspecting the damage the bottle rockets had inflicted.

"Everything okay?" he asked.

"It's burnt pretty bad in a few places," I said, surveying the carpet for scorch marks.

"I wasn't talking about the car."

I looked at my brother. A low, thumping sound began to permeate the air as he spoke. "You know, just because you're going to be off at your fancy college, that doesn't mean..." The thumping noise grew into a roar, louder until it looked as if Dorsey was simply mouthing the words, no sound coming out. He finally stop talking all together and we watched each other and laughed inaudibly until the AirCare chopper lifted off from the roof of the hospital and took to the skies, visibly vibrating the service station's windows.

The sound of the helicopter finally faded and I waited for Dorsey to finish what he was saying. He didn't. He slapped me on the back me and slipped back behind the wheel of his car.

Either out of sheer hubris or some intrinsic need to return to the scene of the crime, Dorsey announced we would make one last circuit of Stratford Road before heading home. When we got there, it was all but abandoned. It was later than I had realized. It felt like cruising through some Twilight Zone version of the Strip, like some kind of fluorescent and neon Monument Valley. The familiar landmarks and establishments, still lit-up but now empty and silent, seemed out-of-place and lonely, like hosts of some big party left behind to clean up and turn off the lights.

A hundred yards from home Dorsey killed the engine and cut the lights. We coasted into the driveway, the crunching of the gravel under our tires the only sounds. The Galaxie rolled to a stop and my brother and I eyed the house for a minute. No lights came on.

We got out and eased the doors shut with our hips until they quietly latched. We walked around the car and propped ourselves up against the trunk. Off to the east, toward town, the sky glowed a dim amber, the low clouds reflecting back the lights of the city. We leaned against that car for what felt like hours, saying nothing, stretching Saturday night out as far as it would go. But the next day came anyhow.

1983
Other Side

Why did the possum cross the road?

Let's forget the necessary burdens of food and reproduction and survival. Disregard instinct. The question is: why not? Why accept stagnation, content to dine upon the refuse of those who presume to be higher up the ladder? (Mine are opposable, too.) Why bid for fickle carnal welcomes with the contempt that familiarity has bred? Is it not better to venture, and to gain? I have tasted the overflow of the carpetbaggers' "developments", cancerous sprawlings that homogenize what came before until it can be found only in memories or caricatures. I have plowed – wait. What was that? Shit, hang on.

Okay. Sorry about that. Where was I? Oh, yeah. I have plowed and harrowed, sown seeds in undiscovered country to the symphony of trilling legions of katydids and crickets. I have seen greener grass. We all come to it in our own way, that gray ribbon that divides. The tall ones wait for the paralyzing lights, then bound and vault. In success, the lights weave and screech. In failure there is paralysis and tufts and red spray, antlers no defense. The gatherers from above descend to scurry, dodge; racing and retracing. For me, the road is but a nuisance, an artificial boundary, to the extent I acknowledge it at all. Where the asphalt conflicts with my journeys, the asphalt is wrong. Tonight's journey has no destination save the other side. And there's your why. The other side. When the time comes, there are no second thoughts. No backward glances. I simply go. I hear a slowly swelling, rabid growl. There are lights down the road, two glowing white circles that grow and grow until they occlude everything else in my field of vision. So often it's the small moments, where if you had taken one more step, or one less, the world would be a much different place. The breeze would smell again like their refuse, and not their machines. The sky would be the color of her fur. I see only the machine's after-image, a flickering zoetrope ghost in the place it, and I, had been only seconds earlier. Soon I hear nothing other than my own halting breaths, and soon not even that.

I'm not playing.

1988

Runs Good

Linda looked in the rearview mirror. The boy was there, waving to her from the garage bay. The old man was standing next to him, not waving. In fact, he was scowling.

"Nice try, asshole," Linda said to the old man's reflection.

He had told her she needed a new tire. "A plug ain't gonna hold," he'd said. "Better off just getting all new *tars*. Ain't another garage between here and Cape Carteret. And you don't want another flat. Not out here. Nothing but *cractor crailer crucks* this time of night."

But she knew better. About the *tar*, at least. Dorsey wasn't good for much else, but he knew cars, and he'd taught her enough to keep assholes like this guy from ripping her off. Her suspicions about the tire had been confirmed when the boy motioned for her to follow him outside when the old man had gotten distracted by one of Barker's Beauties on the tiny black & white TV behind the sales counter.

The boy walked Linda out to the pair of used cars the old man had for sale by the side of the road; an abused late-Seventies Cutlass and a caramel-colored 1972 Datsun 240Z. The Z had *$2,000 Runs Good* written in white shoe polish on the window. The Olds simply said *Make Offer*

The boy looked over his shoulder to make sure the old man was still glued to the television. "Listen, ma'am," he'd begun, his voice hushed. "I can plug your hole."

"Excuse me?"

"I—I mean, no…" The boy had blushed. It looked good on him. "I mean, I can fix your tire. I…I can plug the hole in your tire."

Linda had simply nodded, not offering to help the poor kid get his point across. He was flirting, obviously. He was trying to pretend like he wasn't, like it had been a slip-up, but that was all part of the game. She wondered how many times she'd not recognized moments like this when she was married.

"But it is in a bad spot." They walked to the Galaxie and the boy pointed to the ten-penny nail embedded in the tire. "And I can't guarantee how long it will hold." Then he dropped his voice further still and verified his boss's whereabouts again. "But you don't need a new tire. The old man just wants to make some easy money."

She nodded again.

"But please, ma'am," the boy begged, discernible syllables surfacing every now and then from the bog of his Down East accent. "Whatever you do, don't let on I told you. The old man will fire me on the spot, and I need this job."

She told the boy she understood and while he began to plug her tire she'd gone into the little glass office to give the old man her credit card to pay for the repair. He was still glued to his set, watching the bathing suit-clad girls drape themselves across a shiny new 1988 Chevrolet Celebrity with California emission.

"You know she's from right down the road?"

"Is that right?"

The old man touched the screen, obscuring Dian behind his fat finger. "That one," he breathed. "She's from Jacksonville. At least that's what Joe Daub told me."

No more than five minutes before the boy popped back into the office. "She's beautiful," he said.

"I wouldn't kick her out of bed," the old man said, but the boy hadn't been talking about Dian Parkinson. He was staring out the window at the Galaxie.

"You can have her," Linda said. "I hate that damn thing."

"Seriously?" the boy's eyes flew wide.

"No, not seriously. Well, I'm serious that I hate it. But I'm not serious that you can have it."

The old man asked Linda whose name was on the card, since she didn't look like a Dorsey. Dorsey was her husband, she said, and the old man grunted and ran the card through. What she hadn't told him was that Dorsey was still back in Salisbury and had no idea his wife was on her way to Emerald Isle and he'd never see her again. Dorsey wouldn't know any of that until he got the postcard.

Linda slipped behind the wheel of the Galaxie and checked her lipstick in the rearview. The boy appeared in her open window.

"Which way you headed?" he asked quietly.

"East."

"Well, listen. If you have any more trouble, just pull off the road and hang tight." He checked his watch. "I live out that way about twenty miles and I'll be heading home in a little bit."

Linda thanked the boy and he smiled before walking back to join his boss. She gave the old man a low middle finger where he wouldn't see. Her tires crunched and spat gravel back at him and his young mechanic as she popped the clutch and kicked the gas pedal to the floor. The radials squealed when she hit the baked and faded asphalt of Highway 58 and aimed the Galaxie toward the coast.

Linda watched the tiny gas station until it became a dot on the horizon, receding in her mirror along with everything else that had happened in the past 72 hours. She exhaled for what felt like forever and imagined herself no longer driving a Ford Galaxie, but instead at the helm of a time machine. Back there, in the rearview mirror, was the past. Out there, framed within her dusty windshield was the future. And all she had to do to get there faster was step on the gas. Time-traveling across North Carolina.

She'd left with nothing. Only the dress she had on and her purse. She had spent as much time deciding what to wear as she had making the decision to leave. She'd finally climbed into the attic and dug through three boxes of summer clothes until she'd found this dress. The gauzy white linen one with the spaghetti straps. Dorsey's favorite, because, depending on the light, you could see right through it. Other than the dress, she was wearing only a pair of strappy pumps and perfume, and too much of that.

It wasn't until she limped into that desolate little garage that she first regretted wearing that dress. The old man had looked her up and down like she was the first woman he'd seen in weeks. And maybe she was. He had been damn near paralyzed by her cleavage. But the boy had done his utmost to treat her like a lady, despite the dress. In fact, she thought, the kid deserved a medal for keeping his eyes on hers as she told him about the flat tire. Only once did she catch him looking, the fleetest of glances, when she had bent to pluck a parking lot stone from her shoe. She knew he could see the triangular impression of her thong under the thin dress. She had bought those panties for an situation just like this. Tiny panties. Panties she would have never bought for Dorsey.

The boy was cute enough, Linda thought, in a dirty fingernail kind of way. Blue work pants, greasy rag hanging out the back pocket, dingy shirt with a little patch on the chest that read *Lee*. He had taken five minutes to explain to her that he was Jesse and that Lee didn't work there anymore and hadn't worked there in almost two years, but the old man was too cheap to buy news shirts. John and Ralph before him had also been "Lee" during their brief stints at Highway 58 Motors. She thought about the boy and almost wished she'd been a little sweeter to him.

Dorsey had written her a blank check after all. The boy would've been a good way to cash it. He wasn't even remotely her type; too much like her husband. But there was something about him. She didn't quite know what. Maybe it was his youth. Linda was old enough to be his mother but he was obviously attracted to her, and she liked that. Maybe it was his arms, and how when he'd taken her wheel off, the short sleeves of his work shirt tried to strangle the life out of those ridged biceps. Or maybe it was how nervous he seemed talking to a grown woman. Or maybe it was his hands, running through his hair as he fidgeted. Big hands. Tanned hands. Weathered past their years, like they'd know a tool or two. Whatever it was, she tried to put it out of her mind.

The sky in the rearview was aflame with sunset, the sky ahead darkening. She was running headlong into night, the road like a ribbon laid down between the trees. She hadn't seen a house for miles, nothing but pines and vines and shadows. She wondered where in the hell the boy could live out here.

Wherever we want to go, that's where we'll go, she thought, repeating in her head the words Dorsey had said to her years ago but had long since forgotten. She listened to the singing of the tires, listened to them slap at patches and dips in the pavement, listened to the drone of the big engine. She had tried her best to make Dorsey get rid of this damn thing over the years. Whenever times got a little tight, when a repair got expensive, when he saw a newer, more practical car he liked. But he just wouldn't let go.

"She's getting old," she would say to Dorsey.

"I'm older than this car," he'd say in return. "We ain't old. We're in our prime."

But that was then. She hadn't felt in her prime in a long time. Same for the Galaxie. She used to love this car. Used to love to let Dorsey drive her all around in it. They'd drive for hours sometimes, usually at night, all the windows down. She used to love this car. She used to love Dorsey. There was a time when just the sight of that long red Ford turned her on as much as Dorsey. Now she couldn't stand the sight of either one of them. Just like his damn car, Dorsey was meant for the road. Both needed to be moving onto the next thing. It was what they were made for.

She didn't want the car, but she'd taken it because she knew how bad it would hurt Dorsey to lose it. Worse than it hurt to lose her, she figured. In more ways than one, though, she'd regretted taking it. It had already broken down twice before the flat tire. She'd fixed a pinhole in the radiator hose on the side of the road outside of Asheboro. That one had been easy. When her left rear wheel bearing starting hollering, that one wasn't so easy. She'd made it to a truck stop and sat in the restaurant while the mechanic did his thing. She drank her coffee black because she knew the sugar would wire her for an hour or two then she'd be worthless. And God knew she'd been worthless for too long. Just ask Dorsey.

Suddenly the Galaxie seemed to hiss at her like a snake. Then came the steam, followed by the familiar smell of anti-freeze. *Dammit.* She slowed down and rolled onto the dusty shoulder of the road. She killed the motor and banged her fists

74

against the wheel, trying like hell to think of some reason why this was all Dorsey's fault.

Linda got out and walked around front, took a scornful look at the steam rising from the grill, then opened the hood. A fog rolled out from the engine compartment and enveloped her. She stared for a minute at the radiator hose that had betrayed her yet again, split open like an overcooked hot dog. Linda rested her head against the hood. She couldn't help but wonder if the Galaxie was acting on Dorsey's behalf somehow, if it knew she was running away and was doing everything in its power to keep that from happening. It wasn't too hard to envision the hood closing over her like the mouth of some metal monster and swallowing her whole. She gave the chrome bumper and swift kick.

"Bitch."

She knew there would be no duct taping this one, and there was a pretty good chance Dorsey had an extra hose amongst the junk where the spare should have been. She snagged the keys from the ignition as she rounded the car and opened the trunk. She pushed around Dorsey's toolbox, an old tarp and about two dozen bungee cords. But no radiator hose.

She checked her watch and then checked her odometer. The boy was a half hour and 20 miles in her past. And Emerald Isle was still 50 miles in her future. And she was stuck in the present. She dug in her pocket and fished out the receipt the old man had given her.

Hwy. 58 Motors

Expert Mechanic on Duty

24-Hour Towing

At the bottom was a phone number, but it had been miles since she'd seen any sign of civilization. No way she could walk to a phone. Not out here. And besides, the boy had told her to sit tight. He would come. He would. He had to.

A tractor trailer blasted by, the driver laying on the air horn for good measure, the wind rocking the Galaxie back and forth. The trunk lid creaked and then slammed shut, barely missing Linda's fingers.

"Shit!"

She turned to walk away, but found that she couldn't. She was held tight. There was a split-second of sheer panic. But no one had silently emerged from the woods and descended upon her. Her dress had gotten shut in the trunk when the lid blew closed. She gave a gentle tug, careful not to pull too hard and rip the delicate fabric. It wouldn't budge. She reached for the keys but they were no longer in the trunk latch. She scanned the ground in the dark, patiently and methodically at first and then, when they were nowhere to be found, frantically. She tried to get to her hands and knees, but her bound dress would only let her crouch.

She patted the dirt with the palms of her hands, searching the small radius around her, reaching as far as she could. Nothing. The keys must have fallen into the trunk before the lid closed. She stood and leaned against the car, and let every ounce of air leave her lungs. For a minute or two she considered ripping the dress free. And she wanted to kick herself for not packing anything. But even if she had packed her suitcase it would probably be in the trunk along with her keys. And the last thing she wanted was to give the boy the added satisfaction of seeing her half-naked in a torn-away dress he could practically see through anyhow.

For a moment she felt as if she might cry. But instead, she simply laughed. The boy would be here soon and he could fix it. Even if it meant getting him to jimmy the trunk open and getting towed back to Hwy. 58 Motors and buying a new radiator hose. She still had Dorsey's credit card, after all. She would buy a whole new engine if she had to. It would be okay.

She leaned back against the car, her captor and nemesis, and tried to relax. She thought about the boy again, and kind of wished he had looked at her the way the old man had. She wished Dorsey still looked at her like that. She gave another half-hearted tug at her dress, but it was useless. She looked at the hem, making sure she hadn't already ruined it. And she saw her shining keys wedged in the crevice between the Galaxie's chrome bumper and its body. They had fallen out of the latch and landed there.

The space between the bumper and the car was just wide enough for her to work her fingers in and she could feel the keys with her fingertips. She tried to hook a finger in the key ring but only managed to push the keys further into that gap, out of reach. *Great.* She tried to rotate her body to get a better angle, but her hung dress wouldn't allow it. And when she went to pull her hand free, she found that it too was now held fast. She tried to work her hand down the length of the bumper, hoping to find a place where the gap widened, but her fingers were now as stuck as her dress

77

was. She reached around her body with her free hand, but her arm simply wasn't long enough to offer any help.

She struggled to find a relatively comfortable position to wait for the boy, her options sorely limited. Her trapped fingers kept her from standing upright and her pinned dress prevented her from sitting. Eventually she settled into an awkward squat and rested her weight against the car, and tried not to count the minutes. The road on either side was lined with arrow-straight pine trees, planted in perfect rows. When the wind would blow, they would sway like grass on the savanna. Overhead, the once pale sky had taken on the hue of wet blue ink. Night was coming. She watched the shadows stretch eastward toward the horizon until the sun set.

The low, distant sound of an engine wafted in the breeze. She could hear it well before she could see it. It sounded like it was still five miles away. It was coming from the east, too. The wrong direction. She stood beside the car and waited. Then she decided to duck behind the car and not be seen. The last thing she wanted was for some lonely long-hauler to see her like this, alone and stranded, and decide to stop and "help". *Don't stop. Don't stop.* The sound of the engine drew closer and closer, growing louder by the second until finally it blew by at 70-plus mph, dragging behind it a roiling wake of road debris, dust and hot air.

Come on, Jesse.

Over the next half-hour, two more trucks blasted past, both mercifully oblivious to her predicament. Then a pair of yellow headlights materialized on the western horizon. They seemed to

78

fade in and out of sight, disappearing in the undulating heat waves and wash of exhaust vapors like some kind of motorized mirage. The rumble of the engine grew slowly louder as they approached. Finally the vehicle neared, gearing down with a throaty gurgle, and pulled off of the road behind the hobbled Galaxie.

The door of the wrecker swung open with a rusty groan and the boy dropped to the ground, his worn-out boots hitting with a cloud of dust. He sauntered to her, smiling. He peered around the car at the steam still rising from the engine, then back at the trunk lid that clutched tightly at the hem of its captive dress. *Laugh, motherfucker. I dare you.*

"Yep," he finally offered.

"My keys are behind the bumper," Linda nodded toward them.

"Well, we got a little problem."

"What are you talking about?"

"The old man got a phone call from the bank about five minutes after you left. Seems they've put a freeze on your credit card."

"Oh, that. Listen I can—"

"Which means he didn't get paid for plugging your tire."

"Look, just get me out of here so we can do whatever it is we need to do."

"Well, see, that's problem, ma'am. The old man said he'd fire me if I didn't get cash up front. He said if I saw you to not lay a finger on your car until I collect payment from that little bitch."

the boy turned red. "That's what he said, the old man. That wasn't me calling you that, ma'am. I didn't –"

"I understand. Now, listen to me. Why don't you crawl underneath the bumper here and see if you can reach my keys. My purse is in the trunk. I've got some cash in there."

The boy seemed distressed. "Ma'am, I'm sorry, but the old man told me not to so much as kick a tire without getting paid first."

"Listen, I can't pay you unless you open the trunk."

She watched the boy consider his options. "Ma'am," he started. "Do you really have some money in there?"

She wasn't sure if it was his eyes or his innocence or what, but before she could tell him the lie again, she told him the truth. "No, I don't." She wondered what he was more afraid of, getting caught or crushing the high school sweetheart he was no doubt still charity-dating.

"Ma'am, I'm sorry, I—"

"You can't just leave me out here like this."

"No, ma'am. I can't."

Linda said, "You like this car, don't you?

"Yes, ma'am."

"Give me two grand for it," Linda said.

"It's worth twice that."

"I know. Two-thousand dollars and it's yours."

The boy stared at the car like he'd never seen it before. He rubbed the sandy stubble on his chin. "I don't exactly have it on me."

"Can you get it?"

"I…yeah. I mean…yeah."

"How quick?"

"Maybe not tomorrow, but probably by Monday."

"It's yours," Linda said. "Congratulations," she said, doing her best Dian Parkinson impersonation as she nodded to the car. "You're the proud owner a 1963½ Ford Galaxie 500 XL."

The boy's jaw dropped. He looked at the car, making sure it was real. Linda could've sworn she saw his heartbeat just beneath the embroidered *Lee* on his shirt. She couldn't help but laugh. Another man who liked that damn car better than her.

"Here's what's going to happen. You're going to tow your new car wherever you want, but first you're going to take me back to the station."

The boy simply nodded, never taking his eyes off the Galaxie.

"And you're going to give me the keys to that 240Z sitting by the road."

"Okay."

"And then you'll owe the old man that two-thousand bucks you owe me."

He understood.

"Now," she said. "Get me out of here."

She watched him walk back to the tow truck and open the hood. Like King Arthur drawing out Excalibur, the boy withdrew the dipstick from the grimy engine. It was slick with oil and shining like new, spared the ravages of rust and dust, safe inside the motor. He ran his index finger and thumb down the length of the dipstick, coating them with the thick 40-weight, and then walked back to his stranded motorist. He knelt at Linda's side and slicked up her pinched fingers with motor oil; Round 2 of sleeves vs. biceps. After a few minutes of working, the slippery stuff allowed Linda's hand to come free of the bumper.

Linda massaged the numb fingers as the boy crawled under the bumper and fetched her keys. He got to his feet and opened the trunk, and Linda's dress fell free. She took a deep breath, then planted a kiss on his lips. He smelled like gasoline. Not the watered-down, 90-something octane you got nowadays, Linda thought. But the good stuff you can't get any more. The leaded stuff. The kind that burned clean and pure. Sky Chief. Hi-Test. Neither one of them said a word all the back to Hwy. 58 Motors.

Nine hours later the sun was climbing over the Atlantic. Linda was watching it through the windshield of her Z. It was purring like a kitten.

"Wherever we want to go, that's where we'll go," she said.

1991
Scream If You Wanna Go Faster

Tina Dixon sat next to me in Mr. Barlow's 12th Grade Civics class. She had massive tits and other than that few redeemable qualities. More often than not she was a total bitch; spoiled, selfish and jealous. Her eyebrows were unsymmetrical, one skewed a little higher than the other, which made her look permanently skeptical. She had a wide, flat ass and orange hair that was cut into a shape similar to a Panzer tank commander's helmet. She was also my girlfriend.

Don't get me wrong, I liked Tina, even as it slowly dawned on me I was maybe the only guy at school who did. Even more so, actually. I guess maybe I felt a little sorry for her. Because she wasn't a total bitch all the time. And she had a certain cuteness, I suppose, under the helmet. Plus I had a thing for girls with glasses. And again, there were those amazing tits. Amazing enough that I was able to forgive a wideness and flatness of ass that otherwise would have been a deal breaker.

Tina was the first real girlfriend I'd had. Sure, there had been other girls. Lisa Gates in the 9th Grade. We kissed a lot. I think my thing for braces can be traced back to her. Then there was Britt Summers at the skating rink, parading me around during the Couples Skate while Lisa Lisa and Cult Jam's "Lost in Emotion" blared over the loudspeakers. And of course there was Chrissie Minton, who, in retrospect, tried really hard to get me to bang her behind the Social Studies trailer that afternoon before football practice. But I was only 15 then, and at that age I couldn't discern the unspoken subtleties of "let's go behind the trailer" any more than I could read the original text of the Magna Carta.

The upshot of my lagging distance behind Chrissie in the sexual development department meant that by the time I started dating Tina, I still had a lot to learn. Which, if I'm being honest with myself, leads to the main reason I asked her out in the first place: Her daddy was the preacher man at Victory Baptist Church. And I had heard all the stories about preacher's daughters and knew it was inevitable that within mere nights of first holding Tina's hand in my car I'd be getting the kind of education only a preacher's daughter could give.

It wasn't until we'd been dating a couple of months that I realized Tina wasn't the kind of preacher's daughter I had heard about. She was a Southern Baptist preacher's daughter. The kind that made you get on your knees with her and pray for God's forgiveness immediately after she'd just helped you unfasten her 36D bra. It had taken the better part of four months before I ever even caught a glimpse of my own girlfriends tits, and even then it was an accident, when the shoulder strap on her one-piece snapped halfway down the Wet Banana her daddy had set up for Victory Baptist's Fourth of July "One Nation Under God" celebration. They looked like a pair of water balloons about to burst all over that yellow plastic. She screeched for us not to look, her face beet red as she scrambled to her feet and ran away, but not before me and the entire Youth Ministry got an eyeful. She was struggling futilely to stretch her bathing suit back into place as she ran, her enormous breasts swinging back and forth like Mary and Martha, the bells in Victory's steeple.

Mine and Tina's relationship was a constant tug of war, an unspoken battle of wits, with me springing labyrinthine plots to get Tina naked in my car and her devising insidious countermeasures to foil me. One time I went so far as to drain half of my antifreeze so the engine would run a little hot, forcing us to park and wait until the motor's temperature dropped enough for me to top off the radiator. I suggested we look at the stars from the comfort and warmth of the Galaxie's spacious rear bench, and Tina enthusiastically agreed only to start in with some Bible quotes as she got on her back.

"By the word of the Lord were the heavens made, Jesse," she said, pointing up at a constellation. "They shall perish but thou shalt endure." And I climbed out of the backseat and hey, whad'ya know, looks like she's cooled off.

I'm still not quite sure how it happened, Tina being my girlfriend. I was way more attracted to her sister, Jody. Not that I had a chance with her, of course. For starters she was a year

85

younger than me and no self-respecting Senior would date a Junior. And she had a boyfriend, Billy "The Rocket" Pope, who drove #7 in the Modified division every Saturday night at the stadium. Mean bastard. Plus, Jody was really good-looking, and I hadn't exactly shown a propensity for landing attractive women. Case in point, Tina Dixon.

Even though it pissed Tina off whenever she'd catch me, I couldn't help but stare whenever Jody was around. Aside from a few flirty comments designed solely to make Tina jealous, Jody had never really talked to me. I could count on one hand the number of conversations we'd had. Still, in a lot of ways, I felt like I knew her better than I did Tina. Maybe that was because she was so obvious about who she was. So clear with her intentions. Not like Tina.

Jody was the only girl I masturbated to with any real frequency. Granted, I beat off to everyone from the nice cashier lady at Food Fair to Marlena from "Days Of Our Lives". But they starred in my fantasies periodically at best. They were comets in my masturbation solar system. Jody, though... Jody was the sun. The constant center around which my jerk-off daydreams revolved. She had those same hips her sister had, only Jody had the ass to go along with them. Jody wore really sexy underwear, too. Tina's underwear was cotton, always briefs, usually in white, with the occasional faded pastel thrown in for variety. But Jody wore skimpy bikinis and French cuts in lace or shimmering satin. I knew this because I had seen them scattered across the floor of her bedroom, which happened to be right across the hall from Tina's.

And she had really cool hair. Nothing like the helmet Tina wore. Jody's hair was long, an auburn cascade that tumbled over her shoulders and halfway down her back. Brassy blonde streaks flared from each temple, spiraling through her curls like smoke. She swore up and down they were natural, and I believed her, even if her sister didn't.

There were the stories, too. Everyone in school had heard them. Stories that made the boys seethe with uncontrolled want and the girls sneer with disgust (and more than a little jealousy). I didn't believe those stories. Well, most of them. But like the Rod Stewart stomach-pumping legend, true or not, she had a reputation.

Whenever I was at Tina's house, Jody was usually at the Rocket's trailer or locked in her room. The only time I ever really got to look at her was on the Sunday mornings that Tina talked me into going to church with them. Jody always looked positively delighted to be there. Tina always looked happy, too, but Jody's enjoyment of the proceedings seemed to spring not from the nourishing Word of Christ as delivered by her father, but rather from the bewildering comedy of it all.

Her daddy would tell us to bow our heads to pray and he'd read something from the Good Book. On one side of me, on that cold, hard pew, sat Tina, head bowed as her father begged the Almighty for His blessings that day. Her hands were clasped tight, eyes clenched shut, worshipping her own personal Holy Trinity:

Daddy, God, and Jesus. On the other side of me sat Jody, legs crossed, her shoe dangling precariously from her toes, swaying back and forth like a hypnotist's pendulum as she bounced her knee. I would watch her shamelessly, every time we prayed. I would stare at her feet, her knees, her mouth, the way it hung half-open, as if in some perpetual state of invitation. Every now and then she'd pop open her eyes and catch me looking, and I'd close mine just as suddenly as hers had opened, but not before she could give me that smile of hers, like there was a secret right behind those red lips that was just dying to get out.

While her daddy stood up there and talked about how Jesus died for our sins, all I could think of was committing a few myself. Sometimes I would actually feel guilty enough to close my eyes and try in earnest for a few verses to concentrate on what Tina's father was saying, but I would only hear the parts about sin and lust, and the only thing I could concentrate on was Jody's mortal body. Her daddy would bray relentlessly about sin and fornication and the defilement of the flesh, and all I could think about was how badly I wanted to defile the flesh of his daughters. Either one of them.

He read another verse, I believe he said this one was from Matthew. Or Mark. Maybe it was Michael. Either way, I'm pretty sure it was the one that had tripped up Jimmy Carter. "I say unto you," he bellowed from the pulpit. "Whosoever looketh on a woman to lust after her hath committed adultery with her already in his heart."

Even as her father spoke those words, I lookethed on Jody to lust after her. With maddening clarity I could see her slipping silently off the pew and onto her knees. Her daddy would bleat about whoremongers and adulterers and the vengeance of eternal flame or something. But I could think only of Jody unbuckling my church pants and reaching in to find my erection, then freeing it to coil her tongue around my rod like a serpent.

In the pulpit, Jody's dad would build to an inexorable crescendo, putting the final flourishes on his epic sermon, calling on everyone within the sound of his voice to open up their hearts to Jesus this day. But I was too busy imagining his daughter going down on me.

Rev. Dixon roared, "Repent and be baptized, every one of you, in the name of Jesus Christ for the forgiveness of your sins! And you will receive the gift of the Holy Spirit!"

In my mind's eye, I was pinned to the pew by Jody's mouth, my limbs outstretched, my body splayed like a giant letter *X*. I heard a choir of angels. I saw the heavens part, crepuscular rays of sunlight, just like the ones on the cover of that morning's church bulletin, arraying like a halo around the image of Jody's face.

"In Jesus' name," I could hear her daddy boom. "Amen!"

And I would snap out of it.

***

As I pulled into Nunn's Sand & Gravel I checked on Tina in the passenger seat, hoping to catch a knowing smile on her face but happy enough to see that she wasn't frowning. We crept past the vacant gatehouse and into the lunar landscape of rock piles. We came to rest between two mountains of playground sand, like a space module touching down. A street lamp lit the peaks of the hills and cast shadows that seemed to swallow my car. Had I been ten years younger, those sandy peaks would've seemed a magical destination. Instead, it was the twin peaks beneath Tina's blouse that I gravitated toward.

I shut off the Galaxie's motor and took a minute to scan the valleys of loose substrate, ensuring we were alone. At least two other times I'd driven us to Nunn's only to see the nose of Tommy Cheek's IROC-Z peeking out from behind a pile of pine bark nuggets. But tonight we had the place to ourselves.

I draped my arm across Tina's shoulder. She had taken off her glasses. I thought about asking her to put them on again, but changed my mind. She was almost as pretty as her sister, I decided. Almost. If the light hit her just right. The only other time I could remember having that thought was the night of the prom. I couldn't help but smile when she had walked down the stairs to meet me. My girlfriend was pretty, and I was proud.

The prom was all downhill from there. I had picked her up in the Galaxie despite her thinly veiled suggestions otherwise, like, "I hate your smelly, loud car," and, "I am not going to my prom in that land yacht". For the entire drive she complained about how we had no air-conditioning and the vinyl seats were

90

making her back sweat and how her dress was going to smell like gasoline. She said the wind from the open windows was going to mess up her hairdo, as if anything short of a tornado could budge that Aqua Netted dome. I pointed out the fact that she was the only girl in school who would be arriving at the prom in a classic.

"What a man drives says a lot about him," I'd tried to explain. "It's kinda like that Bugs Bunny cartoon where the doors on the Acme Hat Co. truck opened and all them hats flew out."

"What in the world are you talking about?"

"You know how like when the fedora lands on Bugs, he starts acting like a gangster. And when the old lady's bonnet falls on Elmer's head, he starts acting like an old lady."

"I don't get it."

"I guess what I'm saying is, when you're driving a cool car, you feel cool."

Tina said she'd rather ride in air-conditioning.

The prom's theme was Parisian Nights. The bleachers and tether ball poles had been pushed aside to make room for an ad hoc dance floor in the gymnasium amongst the Art Club's decorations of berets and baguettes. The highlight was watching the faculty after Mrs. Clifford spiked the sherbet punch with Rumple Minse peppermint schnapps (the kind they always advertised in *Rolling Stone* with that awesome airbrushed picture of a scantily clad, broadsword-wielding warrior woman astride a polar bear). There was an ice sculpture of the Eiffel Tower and all of our teachers were slurring their words and staggering around the miniaturized Paris landmark like inebriated, giggling Godzillas.

I would love to say that our prom night ended with Tina giving it up in the back of the Galaxie. That had certainly been my plan. Looking back on it, I realize just how naïve I was.

"I shouldn't have let you drive me out here," Tina said, scowling at the piles of mulch.

"Yeah, but you did. You always do."

"I know."

"Come on," I said, nodding toward the back seat. "Wanna look at the stars?"

Tina climbed into the back and I followed. The "XL" in a 1963½ Galaxie 500 XL doesn't stand for Extra Large, but it ought to. The aft quarters of my Galaxie were roomy enough for Tina and me both to stretch out, the seat as big as a sofa. I reclined as Tina put her warm body next to mine. We gazed up through the Galaxie's back glass at the inky night sky. We said nothing for a while and then Tina began telling me about her day; how much homework Mr. Messick assigned, "Can you believe what Michelle Binkley was wearing today?", that sort of thing. But the only thing on my mind was what beneath the buttons of her blouse. Her mouth was moving but I heard nothing. The sound of her voice slowly evaporated. My peripheral went black until all I could see was her bosom gently rising and falling just under that soft polyester.

I leaned over and pressed my lips against her neck, nibbling at the basin of her collarbone. I moved down onto her

92

chest, pushing her blouse out of the way with my mouth, leaving little kisses as I went, each one lower than the last. I could hear her let out a sigh, but she didn't tell me to stop. I undid the top button and slipped a hand inside her shirt, and then inside her bra, cupping one of her breasts in my palm. I arched my wrist so I could see down her blouse, the light from Nunn's street lamp filtering through the material, mottled and diffuse on her goose-bumped skin. I peered through the shadowy valley of her boobs, down to the plateau of her trembling stomach.

I watched her for a moment, gauging her expression.

"Do you want me to stop?" I said.

She didn't answer at first but then gave a barely noticeable shake of her head.

I rearranged myself until I discovered the proper angle to coil an arm around Tina's body. I ran my hand up her back until I found the industrial-strength clasp that held Tina's dauntless bra in place. Again I paused, waiting for a recrimination that didn't come.

I took a deep breath, closed my eyes, and went to work on that clasp with the precision and delicacy of a safe-cracker. Tina's bra clasps were true marvels of engineering. They were Gordian Knots of chastity. The tensile strength required to restrain breasts of that magnitude was staggering, and Tina's bra clasps invariably consisted of no less than three hooks, each of which presenting its own unique test. The first hook, naturally, was the easiest. I rarely had any problems with it and tonight was no different. With a snap of my finger and thumb, I dispatched of it and watched

Tina's massive bosom relax ever so slightly. The second hook was twice as hard, its responsibilities doubled now that the first hook was off duty. I squeezed my eyes tight and concentrated, visualizing the mechanism in my mind. I gathered one strap in the crook of my index finger and looped my thumb behind the opposing strap, drawing the two together to give myself some slack. I rolled the clasp between my digits, middle finger joining the battle now, until finally I managed to disjoin the stubborn hook from its catch. Tina's breasts slumped and expanded outward visibly. Two down, one to go.

I took a moment to steel myself. I had been given the opportunity to attempt to undo Tina's third bra clasp on only two other occasions, both times fumbling impotently with it for minute upon minute, giving Tina's conscience more than enough time to overtake her hormones. And both times she called the whole thing off and reached back to refasten the top two hooks with absentminded ease as she demanded I drive her back home.

I looked up through the Galaxie's back window and beseeched the heavens for the fortitude my task would require. I caught the final hook between my fingers and began. It was creaking and straining under the load, now doing the work intended for three of its kind. I could feel its power, drawn as taut as cable steel. I tried to detach the hook with the same snap-and-twist maneuver I'd found success with on the first two hooks, but it was useless. I simply didn't possess the finger strength. I turned my hand over, trying to find a mechanical advantage like I remembered from Mr. Poe's Physics class. I could feel it working;

94

I could feel the hook slipping its bonds. Then, as if the clasp's configuration had morphed somehow, I was stuck. I came at it from yet a different angle, refusing to surrender, the bra likewise. Beads of sweat were forming on my forehead, the weight of concentration creating furrows for my perspiration to trace. I redoubled my efforts, ignoring my dignity and reaching behind Tina with my other hand. Bordering on panic, desperate to unfasten her bra before she changed her mind, I took the clasp in both hands and wrestled with it. I sawed at it, wringing and strangling it, until somehow, miraculously, it came unhitched. With a great heave and sigh, Tina's breasts were liberated.

I was so excited I was quivering. How many nights had I lied awake in my bed, imagining this exact moment, dreaming of it? How many times had I pictured it, envisioning every possible scenario, every situation? And now it had finally arrived. Here. Now.

I shifted my weight on the car seat, trying to alleviate some of the pressure building between my legs. I could hear Tina's breath becoming ragged. "Go ahead," she whispered.

I thought of Ponce de Leon. I thought of Magellan. This was the furthest I'd ever been with Tina. I was in uncharted waters. I unbuttoned and opened her blouse, revealing her massive tits in all their naked glory.

"No," Tina said suddenly, rising from the seat and gasping for air as she clutched her shirt closed. "Wait."

"What?" I was panting, my heart threatening to burst from my chest at any moment.

Tina quickly shuffled, struggling with her bra until it was back in place. "This is wrong. We can't."

"Of course we can," I pleaded.

"No, no," she said. "It's just not right." She began to tell me what the Lord said about love and sin and sex and marriage, but I didn't hear a damn word of it. "Come on," she said as she got to her knees in the floorboard. She had me by the hand, tugging at me like a child. I didn't budge. I simply sat and stared out the Galaxie's window at the giant mounds of sand, beckoning me to come climb them.

Tears welled in Tina's eyes and she began to beg Jesus to forgive us while pledging her unconditional love to Him. I'd had enough. I began to crawl back into the front seat.

"Wait," Tina said from her knees. "Don't go. Please."

Something in her eyes made me stop, something about the way she said please. Like maybe there was still a chance. Maybe there was still hope. Like maybe if we prayed just right, we might find some kind of loophole in the Word. We might find some kind of divine exemption for hardship.

I let Tina pull me into the back seat. By the time she'd said "Amen" her eyes were dry and she even had a little smile on her face. Jesus still loved her, apparently. Despite the fact that she came this close to letting me play with her titties.

"You understand, right?" she said, laying her head on my shoulder. And still I thought it all might be some kind of code for, *Jesus says it's cool. He was a horny teenager once himself.* Kind of a 'beg forgiveness, not permission' thing. I figured the embers were still hot, all I had to do was fan the flame.

"You know how rare you are?" I said.

"Don't even try it."

"I'm serious. It's your hair."

"I know you hate my hair."

"What?" My mock indignation almost convinced even myself. "I love your hair." I moved closer.

Tina eyed me cautiously. "Go on."

"The gene for red hair is recessive. Not just to dark hair, but to blonde hair, too."

"And?"

"And since neither of your parents are redheads, they had only a one-in-four shot at having a redheaded kid. I learned that in Mrs. Harper's class."

I could see she was turning that over in her brain, slowly coming to the realization that she was the special one, not Jody. At least as far as hair color was concerned.

Tina looked at me. "You really think I'm rare?"

I slung my arm around her neck and squeezed her arm. "Absolutely." I leaned in to kiss her and let my hand slip under her collar.

"What do you think you're doing?" she said, while at the same time dropping her shoulder to give me better access.

"Appreciating a rarity." It was terrible line, but I didn't care. I nuzzled my face under her orange helmet and nibbled at her earlobe. Heat radiated from her body. I worked my hand inside her bra and clamped onto a breast. She didn't protest and I eased my hand deeper still into her blouse and clutched her other breast.

"No. Don't," Tina panted suddenly, swatting my hand away and catching her breath.

"Come on. Please," I moaned. It was pathetic.

"Tina was shaking her head vehemently. "No. No."

I planted my hands on the upholstery and stared at the headliner, my jaw clenched.

She said, "Let me ask you something." She waited for me to grant permission, but eventually realized I wasn't going to and asked me anyhow. "Would you want our first time to be like this? Sneaky? Hiding behind a bunch of piles of gravel?"

"Jesus, Tina, it's not like I was hoping we'd actually *do it* right here and now," I said incredulously, even though that's exactly what I had hoped.

"Good, because that's not how I've got it pictured."

"That's the problem, Tina," I said. "You don't have it pictured at all. If it were up to you, we'd never do it."

"That's not true. I just believe we should save it for our wedding night."

"You know what I think? I think you're scared."

"I am." She was trying like hell to generate some tears. "I'm scared of what Jesus will think."

"I'll tell you what Jesus is thinking. Jesus is thinking, 'For God's sake, woman, at least let the poor boy cop a feel."

Tina gasped. "Take that back."

"Nope."

Tina sat in stunned silence for a few minutes. Finally she looked at me. "What if we did it? Okay? What if I finally gave in and gave you what you wanted?" I waited for the rest of it. "What if it's the worst experience of our entire lives? What if I hate myself for doing it? What if I hate you for making me?"

"God, Tina, you make it sound like rape."

"Don't you want that magical first time to be on the most special night of our lives? The night we enter into holy matrimony in the eyes of the Lord?"

Tina paused to let what she was saying sink in. I shrugged my shoulders.

"Are you willing to risk Hell eternal for it?"

"Yeah, sure."

Tina stared in disbelief. Suddenly she clambered into the front seat, flopping down and staring out the window. Arms crossed and foot tapping, she waited for my regretful admission of guilt and wrongness. When she finally realized it wasn't coming, she simply said, "Take me home."

***

We rode back to Tina's house without saying a word, the only sound was the trusty rumble of the 390. About a hundred yards from her driveway I killed the motor and the headlights. We had enough momentum to carry us around back, where we silently coasted to a stop. I watched Tina as she crossed in front of the car, the parking lights throwing her shadow into infinity. She stopped a few steps shy of her back door and looked back at me. "Well?"

"Well, what?"

"You coming in or what?"

And again, just like that, the fire of hope was stoked.

We slipped inside the house and I stealthily followed Tina through the back porch, through the kitchen, lit only by the light in the exhaust hood over their old burnt-orange stove, and down the hallway.

My eyes were fixed on Tina's wide, flat ass, not where I was going, and I punted Chico's food bowl down the hallway. The aluminum bowl skidded noisily across the hardwood floor, tiny pellets of dog food scattering through the air and landing in a hailstorm of crunchy kibble. The bowl bounced off the front door with a clang and began to spin wildly, spiraling ever faster and tighter, like a penny. Or a figure skater. Faster it spun, the *wow-wow-wow-wow-wow* of the metal bowl growing louder with each revolution until finally it came to rest and the house fell silent again.

Tina turned to glare at me, the whites of her eyes almost glowing in the dim hallway. Then came the *fip-fip-fip* of Pomeranian paws on wood, and Chico materialized at the mouth of the hall, twitching like a possessed dust mop. Upon sighting me, Chico erupted in a shower of shrill barks, each staccato burst seemingly driving the little bastard backwards across the smooth floor.

"Tina!" came a bellow from her parent's bedroom on the far side of the house.

"Sorry!" Tina called back, shuffling to the end of the hall and scooping the dog into her arms. She snap-extended her arm and pointed towards the stairs that led up to hers and Jody's bedrooms. With a jerking nod, she mouthed the words "Go!" and "Now!"

I quickly climbed the stairs and ducked into Tina's room, pushing the door halfway closed behind me. I could hear the muffled sounds of Z93 coming from Jody's room, just across the stair landing. Her door was cracked, and I could see Jody's bare feet dangling off the foot of her bed, swaying to the beat of Bryan Adams singing "(Everything I Do) I Do It For You". Then came the sounds of Tina sweeping up the dog food and refilling Chico's bowl. After a few minutes I could hear Tina padding up the stairs. She glided inside, closing the door behind her. She stood and stared at me for a long while, her hands on her hips.

As hard as she tried, she couldn't fight the grin forcing the corners of her lips into a curl. At the first sign of her smile, we both burst into a fit of stifled giggles and she slung her arms around my neck and kissed me. "I'm sorry," she whispered.

"Me too," I lied.

At that exact moment, Tina's mom's scratchy voice came from somewhere downstairs. "Tina? Who's with you?"

Tina and I froze.

"Tina?"

"Yes, Ma," Tina called back.

"What are you doing?"

"Nothing, Ma."

"I heard a boy's voice, Tina."

"It was Bryan Adams , Ma."

"Who?"

"Bryan Adams."

There was a confused pause, and then, "There's a boy up there with you?"

Tina explained, "It's the radio, Ma."

"Damn jungle music," I could hear Tina's mom mutter. If they didn't wear a sweater vest or hadn't appeared at least twice on Lawrence Welk, it was jungle music. "Turn that foolishness off and go to sleep!"

"Okay, Ma."

Tina and I remained frozen, listening for the sound of her mother shuffling up the steps to check on her, but we never heard it.

I took Tina by her wrist and pulled her to me, nibbling at her lips and feeling for the top button of her blouse. She pushed herself away and stared at me like I'd grown a second head.

"Are you serious? You just don't give up, do you? I can't believe you."

I went to her, reaching again for her button.

She deftly sidestepped me. "Even if I wanted to – "

"You do want to. You know you do."

"Even if I did want to, my parents are downstairs. My sister is just across the hall."

102

"Let's get out here, then. Let's go for a ride."

"What? You just brought me home. You're not taking me for another ride. We're not going anywhere."

"You know you want to."

"No," she said. Tina stop evading me and stood her ground. She stared at me and took a long, deep breath, the kind you take right before you're getting ready to break some really bad news. "No. I don't. This is wrong. This whole night was wrong."

I watched her as she turned and dropped to her knees beside her bed. "Dear Lord," she began, eyes clenched, fists clasped.

"Jesus," I sighed and turned to walk out.

Tina stopped in mid-prayer. "Where are you going?"

"Home."

"What? Why?" She trotted to me and began with the tugging again. "Wait," she said and pulled the Holy Bible from her nightstand. With practiced precision, she instantly flipped to the exact passage she was looking for. "1 Corinthians 10:13," she started. "'There hath no temptation taken you but such as is common to man: but God is faithful, who will not suffer you to be tempted above that ye are able; but will with the temptation also make a way to escape, that ye may be able to bear it.'" She looked at me and smiled. "I think that promise means just what it says, that God will provide a way out of every temptation. If he didn't, then how could he punish us for giving in?"

"I can't take this anymore." I opened the door. "You want it just as bad as I do, and you know it."

"Let's don't have this argument again," she said.

"Don't worry. We won't."

Tina simply stared at me as I walked out of her room. I pulled the door closed and waited on the landing before walking down the stairs, listening for two things; one, the tandem snoring of Tina's mom and dad; and two, the sound of Tina padding to the door to plead with me to stay. I only heard one of those things.

I carefully made my way down the stairs, the dual chainsaw noises coming from down the hall letting me know that Tina's parents were fast asleep. Just as I reached the bottom, I heard the sound of a door creaking open upstairs. I paused.

Then came a whisper. "You can take me for a ride."

I smiled and turned around. At the top of the stairs stood not Tina, but her sister, Jody. She was standing there, wearing only a pair of mint green satin panties and a tight white tank top. Her hair jutted in all directions. She looked positively delicious. If God was providing me a way out of this temptation, He had hidden it well.

Not allowing myself time to weigh the consequences, I skipped back up the stairs, stopping at the next to last tread, which put me at eye level with Jody. With that mouth of hers she gave me the most devilish smile I'd ever seen.

She put her mouth to my ear. "Give me five minutes." Her breath was humid. My hard-on triumphantly returned.

"My car's out back," I mouthed, barely making a sound.

Jody nodded and turned and disappeared into her bedroom, pushing the door shut behind her. I could hear the onion-skin pages of the Bible being flipped through in Tina's room.

I glided back down the stairs, through the hallway and kitchen, and out the back door. I trotted across the dewy grass and between the gravel mountains until I got back to my car. I slid inside and waited, wrapping both hands around the wheel to keep them from shaking.

Five minutes was an eternity. I counted off every second in my head. The first five minutes came and went. Then another. And just as it slowly began to dawn on me that Jody had possibly played the cruelest trick ever on me, she appeared from behind a giant mound of bark chips. She was barefoot and had squeezed into a pair of faded cut-off Levi's, so short the front pockets peeked out from the behind frayed hems. She was wearing a Billy Pope t-shirt that used to be red but had faded to pink and the cotton was worn tissue-thin. She had it on inside-out, *EPOP "TEKCOR EHT" YLLIB* arcing across her chest.

She made her way to my car slowly, watching the ground, planning her every step, avoiding the jagged gravel when she could, sometimes setting a bare foot down on one and drawing it back to step elsewhere. She finally made it and slid into the passenger's seat, the scent of baby oil following her in. She used her toes to clear out a space for her feet among the wrenches, rags and Channellocks on the floor. Her candy apple lips were the exact same shade as my car. My erection pushed against my jeans almost painfully. I wanted nothing more at that moment to leap on her, pin her body under mine, tear away her clothes…

"Drive," she said.

The Galaxie's engine came growling to life and Jody and I wove our way through the rock piles until we got back to the asphalt.

"Right," she said, and I turned right.

We drove away from her house, blasting down the razor-straight stretch that headed out of town. I wanted to ask where we were going, but it didn't really matter. I couldn't keep my eyes off her. The air rushed in, hot and thick and damp, making that long hair lash about her face, those blonde streaks zapping all around like bolts of lightning. She was everything her sister wasn't; wild, beautiful, free and dangerous. I'd never wanted anything so badly in my whole life.

We left behind the streetlights and houses of town, the only signs of life the occasional blinking traffic signal. In between was only blackness, split down the middle by a receding ribbon of grey asphalt, lit only by the Galaxie's headlights. We drove for miles. There wasn't a soul on the road except us. For all we knew, we could have been the only people in the whole world, driving the last car on Earth.

"Faster," Jody said suddenly. I eased the pedal down and watched the speedometer needle creep past 70. A cacophony of sounds filled the car; the wind whistling, the tires singing and slapping at patches and dips in the asphalt, the 390 droning reliably, the pipes broadcasting through the countryside.

"This is a nice car," she said. "I gave my first blowjob in a car like this."

My heart jumped into my throat. I'd had maybe three conversations ever with my girlfriend's sister, and now here she was, talking to me about her virginity and the loss thereof. The world had caromed on its axis. Maybe it was the blackness of the night, or Jody's perfume, or the sound of the motor. Most likely it was the combination. Whatever it was, a wave of déjà vu washed over me and I was instantly transported to the Dixie Classic Fair, just a year ago. Tina and I were riding the Himalaya, its galloping centrifugal force pressing me against the side of the car. Pressing Tina against me. My mind swirled with the possibilities. I remembered the digit-deficient carnie commanding his dizzy charges, "Scream if you wanna go faster!"

"Of course, that car couldn't pull a sick whore off the toilet," Jody said, back in the present. "This one's fast. I can tell." I doubted she even knew what kind of car she was riding in beyond the fact that it was a Ford. But I didn't care.

She went on. "Daddy made Tina take me with her on her first date. Guy's name was Donnie, maybe. Vonnie? Nah, Donnie. Anyhow, I guess Daddy thought if Tina had her little sister along nothing bad would happen." Jody let out a little laugh. "Like Saint Tina would do anything bad. Of course, you know all about that." I could only nod.

"Anyhow, Donnie's folks wouldn't let him go unless his older brother came along. Tina got stuck with her little sister, Donnie got stuck with his big brother." Then, as if only to herself,

107

Jody said, "Maybe the brother's name was Vonnie." And then she was talking to me again. "Donnie had just gotten his license, so no way in hell was he not driving on his first date. But Donnie didn't have a car. So he begged his dad to let him borrow his. Of course, me and Vonnie got stuck in the backseat together." Jody glanced over her shoulder at the backseat of my car. "And that's a comfy backseat."

"We went to the movies. 'Rambo III'. We all wanted to see 'Cocktail', but you know Daddy. No way was he letting us go see a movie about alcohol. Well, the movie sucked, naturally. And on the way home ol' Vonnie was flirting pretty hard. Telling me how pretty I was, how sexy I was. He said, 'You know, sexiness is ten percent looks, ninety percent attitude.' Keep in mind I was maybe 14 at the time. In Vonnie's defense, my mascara made me look at least 16. Anyhow, of course Tina was hearing all this from the front seat, and getting pissed. You know how she is."

Again I nodded.

"Anyhow, Vonnie takes my hand and the bastard sticks it right down his pants. Right down the front of his pants. And he's hard. And it felt huge. I had seen a few dicks before, but never held one. And I had no idea what to do, so I just kinda held it, you know? Like I was holding his hand or something." A burst of laughter escaped Jody. "So Vonnie reaches in his pants with me and starts to jack himself, but using my hand, showing me how he wanted it done."

"Donnie drives us home, back to my house, and he and Tina get out. Tina won't even look at me. As soon as Donnie and

Tina are in the house, Vonnie pulls it out. And it's even harder than before. I tried a couple of different grips before he finally lost his patience with me and pushed my head down. I resisted at first, more out of instinct than anything, but he was a lot stronger than me and I wasn't really fighting anyhow."

Jody got quiet and stared out the window for a moment, as if accessing the memories. "Drive faster," she finally said, and I did. "He told me a good blowjob was ten percent technique, ninety percent enthusiasm." She laughed, just slightly, to herself. "I remember thinking that this one was going to be zero percent technique."

I simply drove and listened, transfixed, like a boy listening to a ghost story around a campfire. I had to remind myself to breathe. The speedometer needle was hovering around 90.

"I could feel him watching me. And I loved that. I wanted him to see what I looked like, what my face looked like. I wanted to burn that image into his brain. I tried to imitate the girls I'd seen on cable television, thinking it would make me seem like a pro, like a woman who knew what she was doing, not a pretender obsessing over the details: Was I using enough tongue? Was I moaning loud enough? Should I stick my ass out?

"He was begging me not to stop. He was telling me how good I was, how beautiful I was. But I didn't care if he thought I was beautiful or not. Only that I was good. He called me 'Baby' a lot. I think it was because he couldn't remember my real name. I remember he asked me if I liked sucking his cock. And I told him

I did. But I didn't like it half as much as I liked the look on his face when I told him I did."

The wind from a passing tractor-trailer crashed against the windshield, buffeting the whole car and startling me so bad I almost jumped out of my seat. The Galaxie seemed to be floating, like we were flying just a few inches above the asphalt, like gravity was gone. I halfway expected to see my Channellocks pirouetting in midair between Jody and me. I nudged the wheel to make sure our tires were still touching the road.

"At one point I looked up and saw Tina and Donnie, watching us through the car window. They'd come back out to check on us, I guess. Tina was staring right at me." Jody watched the black landscape for a moment. "I'm sure Tina expected me to stop then. I'm sure she expected me to be mortified and hide my face and run away into the house in shame. But I didn't. I didn't stop. Hell, if anything I worked even harder. I wanted to give him the best blowjob he'd ever gotten. I know for a fact I didn't. The one I gave him the next night was twice as good, I'm sure of that. But right then, with my goody-goody sister staring at me, I wanted to give ol' Vonnie the blowjob of his life. The one he'd compare every other one to. The stuff of legend." She laughed a little at the sound of that. "I tried to give him the blowjob he'd relive every time he jacked off. I wanted to make sure he never jacked off to anybody else ever again."

The Galaxie's right front dipped off the pavement and onto the shoulder in a noisy hail of gravel before I yanked us back onto the good side of the white line.

110

"He was bucking up off the car seat. I let him gag me because I knew it would make my eyes water and make my mascara run. And I knew that would drive him crazy." I closed my eyes for a split-second and pictured Jody's face, cheeks streaked with black watercolor tears.

"I tried to watch his face and look into his eyes and share our moment, you know? But it wasn't like that. Which was fine, really. It was better that way. He had to take it from me. I couldn't just give it. Or else it wouldn't have been what he needed. And I needed to be what he needed."

I felt lightheaded.

"I could feel his body trembling," Jody said. "He was going to come. I was going to make him. And I wanted him and his brother and my sister all to know that. He let out this kind of muffled moan. More of a purr, really. It was pitiful." She laughed again, louder this time.

She sat and didn't say anything else for a minute or two, as if letting everything she'd told me sink in. When I finally looked over at her, Jody was smiling at me. I suddenly had the feeling that somehow she had expected this, that she knew the whole time this would be the outcome; her in control of me. I wanted to hate her for her arrogance. More than that, I wanted to hate myself for wanting this. But I did want it. More than even Jody could know. I tried to think of her as the manipulative little slut she was, but all I could see was the confidence of someone what knew what she wanted and wasn't afraid to take it, and I was envious of that. It was like watching someone intentionally run a red light. I felt that same sense of shock that someone would so brazenly break the law, then felt an admiration for the person who didn't let the color of a light bulb tell them what to do.

Jody reached into the pocket of her cut-off jeans and pulled out a crumpled pack of Winstons. She lit one, the orange flicker of her lighter dancing across the ceiling of the car. She exhaled the thick smoke and said, "You don't mind, do you?"

I shook my head. I could see Jody out of the corner of my eye in the blue shadows, intermittent bands of light sweeping across her bare legs as we passed under streetlamps.

"So how about it?" she said suddenly. "Do you like having your dick sucked?"

I shifted in my seat, partly out of nervousness and partly to accommodate my aching erection. I was almost nauseous with excitement. My legs couldn't be still, my knees opening and closing like bellows. I avoided Jody's face even as I could feel her studying mine. She had said it loud enough to be heard over the engine and wind but I faked otherwise, buying a few precious seconds to formulate a coherent response.

"What?" I asked ridiculously.

Jody laughed. "Relax. It's okay. I'm not going to bite."

If I had any doubts about whether I was going to let this happen, they had long since vanished. I thought suddenly of how, when I was a boy, I couldn't see over the dash of my momma's car and every time we approached the bridge over the river, the surrounding landscape dropped off and there would be seemingly nothing else around, like we were about to drive off the edge of

112

the Earth. And I would be scared to death, because we wouldn't slow down at all. We would just barrel headlong into that nothingness, and I would close my eyes and pray that the bridge was really there. And it would be there every time. This is what that felt like.

Jody smoked her cigarette in silence for a mile or two. I tried desperately to make some sense of how I got here, with my girlfriend's little sister naked in my car talking to me about oral sex. But it was useless.

She inhaled the last of her Winston and then flicked the lipstick-rimmed butt outside in a shower of sparks "Turn here," she said. "Next right."

I took the next right, and all the other lefts and rights she gave until we were deep within Brightstar Mobile Home Park. Scattered amongst the mildewed double-wides with their dilapidated redwood decks and fake stone skirting was the occasional empty lot, providing plenty of poorly-lit hiding places.

"Here," Jody said, pointing to a gravel driveway. This lot had a trailer. With the lights on I could see the #7 Modified on jack stands in the back yard. "The Rocket lost his license last week or else he could've picked me up himself."

I had simply been her ride. Nothing more. And I could feel that realization pushing me down into the seat. It was like lying in the bathtub after all the water had drained out; like I weighed twice what I had before.

Jody hopped out as soon as the car was stopped. She leaned back into the window, crossing her forearms on the door. I

113

couldn't bring myself to look at her. I was too afraid she'd see my dejection and find it pathetic, or funny, or embarrassing, or any number of reactions a girl like her might have to a guy like me thinking he ever had a shot. Instead I sat, hands at 10 and 2, and stared at the speedometer needle lying on *0*.

"Well," she finally said. "Thanks for the lift."

She waited in the window for another moment until she realized we really had nothing to say. Jody patted the door as she stood and walked to her boyfriend's mobile home. I watched her until she disappeared inside, the screen door banging shut behind her.

I backed out of the driveway and followed my mental breadcrumbs back to the main road.

Tina's bedroom light was still on when I rode past her house.

2042

The Last Galaxie on Earth

My momma named me Earlie, which I always felt was kinda fucked up. Not because it was a bad name. I was named after my daddy and I was proud of that. The problem was that I didn't feel early. I felt late. By about half a century. Had I been born when I belonged, I'd be wrenching on something with a V8, not the soulless toasters they pass off as cars these days. I looked around me at the garage I'd been working in since I was 22. The bays at Cale's Auto were all occupied by Slate, Smoke, Gunmetal, Flint, Ash, Cinder and Oatmeal transportation appliances. The mechanical equivalents of corduroy jumpers.

I dropped a lithium ion battery array in place and affixed its safety cover, realizing with a glance that the 10mm wrench I'd used for the batteries wouldn't work for the plastic box that hid their shame. I turned to my tool chest and plucked a 9mm from the top drawer.

"Why can't they make this shit all the same size?" I asked Ms. August on the Snap-On Tools calendar taped inside the lid of my tool chest. I tightened the bolts that held the battery cover. "I swear, honey, next year at this time we're going to be on the beach," I said to the bikini-clad girl straddling the giant Phillips-head screwdriver.

Cale, who was replacing the potentiometer on a '37 Taurus next to me, didn't even look up. "That's what you said to Miss July."

"And that bitch ran off and left me the last day of the month."

I've been an auto mechanic since I was about seven years old. I can remember sitting in the driveway and Daddy dumping out a bucket full of engine parts and making me tell him what each thing was called and what it was supposed to do and what happened when it didn't. My daddy, and Big Earl before him, had made their livings knowing these things, and I would, too. But Americans weren't allowed to drive cars with internal combustion engines anymore, and when the Gore Act passed, my old man was too close to retirement to fool with learning about potentiometers and inductive paddles and pulse controllers, and had said, quite literally, fuck it.

After Daddy had called it quits, it wasn't long until Cale sold out to Current Auto, the national chain of electric car repair shops, with the stipulation that he be allowed to stay on as a technician until he decided to join Daddy in retirement, which wouldn't be long. They simply came in and bought what Daddy had spent a lifetime to build, and somehow felt the same sense of accomplishment.

116

Before selling out, Cale made sure the Current brass agreed to keep me on the payroll. What they didn't agree to, however, was my dirty blue jeans. Or my dirty t-shirt. Or my calendar of dirty girls posing suggestively with oversized vises and wrenches and C-clamps. And they'd made me take them down. They made me cut my hair. They made take my radio home, the one that could still pick up the public domain station. They'd let me keep my old tool chest but only after threatened disciplinary action and only if I scraped off the dozens of high-performance stickers that adorned it. I'd hated to do it, if for no other reason than the years it had taken me to accumulate those stickers. I would miss my Hooker heart and my Clay Smith woodpecker and my Mobil Pegasus. But those companies were long gone anyhow, legislated into extinction. The things they advertised – exhaust headers, camshafts, motor oil – were things used on internal combustion engines. Dangerous, polluting things. They made Cale take down his *Vintage Exotic Cars* calendar for the same reason. The Current Auto brass didn't want their customers associating the Current brand with those things. They wanted their customers to associate Current with cleanliness, safety and courtesy. And they gave me a uniform with an oval patch sewn on the chest that read *Earlie*.

They sent us a manager. A kid, really. Brayden Podner. Fresh out of Current University (that's what they called their 90-day training program). He'd spent a couple of months at a Current Auto Parts store, learning how to do payroll, scheduling and how to ring customers up when they couldn't figure out how to work the self-checkout. He'd pulled a muscle in his back stocking jugs of washer fluid. He learned the ins and outs of air fresheners, fuzzy dice and press-on hood scoops. What he didn't learn was anything that had to do with repairing automobiles. And now he was running an automobile repair shop.

"Got that battery changed yet, Earl?" Brayden called out. He was one step into the garage, which was just about as far as he liked to go.

"Wrapping it up now, Mr. Podner." I liked calling him Mr. Podner for a couple of reasons. For starters, Brayden hated it. Also, it seemed ridiculous to call a man half my age 'Mister', which struck me as indicative of the larger ridiculousness of this kid running Cale's Auto. Plus, it made me sound like some old cowboy referring to his young, overzealous sidekick as "Mr. Partner".

"You should've had it finished half an hour ago," Brayden said, no doubt having just referenced Current's labor guide. "A battery array change takes 75 minutes."

"Not if you ghost their hard drive it don't."

"That's an additional service. You should know this by now. We don't ghost hard drives for free, Earl."

"We used to," I said, making myself stop short of adding, "When Cale ran things around here". The last thing Cale needed was to have his name dragged into this.

"You used to do a lot of things around here you don't anymore," Brayden said as he spun on his heel and retreated to the office.

118

I counted to ten and dropped my 9mm back in the drawer with a clang. I wiped my hands and looked again at Miss August. I could see her on the beach with me. Varadero, maybe. Or Cayo Coco. I could hear the rhythmic crash of the breakers, the hiss of the foam. Maybe I could hop on that big screwdriver with her and paddle to Cuba.

***

I lived in a little town called Ronda, in the heart of what used to be bootlegging country a century earlier. I worked on those electric shavers on wheels till 5:30 every day, then went home to my trailer and went straight to sleep even before the sun sank below the Brushy Mountains. The people who first took to these hills carved roads and livings out of them. Those roads eventually crossed and made towns like North Wilkesboro and Moravian Falls and Ronda. And back in the woods, away from the towns and roads, the men of those hills quietly squeezed a living from hot copper tubes. When the liquor became illegal, the Revenuer Man came tromping through the woods with his axe. The hounds bayed and the fox ran. The fox ran in '40 Ford Coupes and '51 2-door sedans, hot flatheads under the hoods. The fox ran his liquor down from the ridges of Wilkes County, down to Winston-Salem, High Point, Salisbury. And the hounds couldn't catch that fox.

The stills were long gone. So were the men who worked them. But the hounds were still here. They still bayed and chased.

Only now they chased gasoline, not corn mash. I'd just about give my left nut for a gallon of either.

My Halo went off at midnight, just like it did every night, and I dragged my ass off the couch and pulled on the jeans Brayden Podner said I couldn't wear anymore. Like I did every night, I grabbed a slice of pickle pimento loaf from the fridge and stumbled out to my 2032 Prius. It was another hot one. They were calling for an overnight low of 26°C, but it had a long ways to go. I propped opened the Prius's hatch, opened my battered Craftsman toolbox and flipped the lunchmeat onto a crumpled tube of gasket sealant. As I flopped into the driver's seat, the Blink terminal in the steering column detected the Halo on my wrist and accessed my driving record in the DOT database, making sure that it hadn't changed since I shut the car off six hours earlier. Infrared spectroscopy sensors mounted to the rearview mirror begin sniffing the air, making sure it couldn't smell alcohol or nicotine on my breath.

A modulated and halfway smartass female voice came from my dash. "In the interest of national security, this commute may be monitored by local and/or federal transit authorities." I listened to Ford Motor Company's death/injury disclaimer and liability waiver, and verbally accepted each, after which my car finally allowed me to press the start button.

I drove down the twisting dirt road away from my trailer, the car making no sounds except for the voice in the dash. It updated me on the day's terror and urban civil unrest threat levels.

"Goddammit," I said. "Tools."

120

"Tools," the car's voice repeated back to me.

"Options. Location. 28670," I said. "For the fortieth fucking time."

The dashboard went on with its reports, leaving out anything about big cities, sticking to just the air quality, water quality and UV forecasts.

The dash voice was saying, "The National Weather Service's Space Weather Prediction Center has issued a geomagnetic storm warning for Saturday, August 23, 2042, expected to begin at approximately 12:30am…"

I tried not to pay attention to it. I had no idea why in the hell I needed to know about space weather, or any of that shit, but I also knew there was no way to shut that bitch up. Not without snipping a wire or pulling out a fuse, and I'd learned at WCC that it was illegal to screw with your onboard communications system. I'd seen enough confused customers come in to Cale's wondering why their car wouldn't start to know what happened if you did.

There were no Amber Alerts or Silver Alerts that night. Even still, my car didn't shut up until I was pulling into Baby Dolls.

I liked Baby Dolls, despite all the laws. All-nude had gone away first. Then came the pasties. Then they banned clear pasties. (Dancers at the upscale clubs got artsy with their pasties. Burlesque-style tassels, flower petals and glittery seashells could all be seen hiding nipples at the fancier establishments in town. Baby Dolls, thank the Lord, was anything but upscale.) Then they banned flesh-colored pasties. Then came diameter requirements on the pasties. (Of course, the federally mandated four-inch circles couldn't contain Sapphire's pancake-sized areolas.) Once the nipples had been safely tucked away, the decency brigade had turned their disapproving eyes on the bottoms. The g-string was the first casualty, followed quickly by width standards for thongs. If during one of his frequent surprise visits, the county health inspector judged any dancer's thong to be less than the width of two fingers at its narrowest, Lanier, Baby Doll's owner, would face fines of up to 1,000 amero and that particular dancer would be cited and sent home for the night. (But not before a top-of-his-lungs berating by Lanier if he was feeling generous, termination if he was not; in his office if you were lucky, in front of the customers if you were not.) But the main reason I like Baby Dolls was that the girls weren't skinny like the ones at Filly's.

The parking lot was pretty empty even by Baby Dolls' standards. There were only a handful of cars, a few of what passed for Harleys these days, and a tractor trailer, an old one with the hybrid trailer assist. I walked through the club's main entrance, into the cramped vestibule, and held my Halo up to a wall-mounted Blink terminal. My Baby Dolls membership number, criminal record and the bank account I had on file were automatically transferred. I tapped the screen where it said to and acknowledged that I understood the nature of the establishment its activities and that I hereby released Baby Dolls, LLC, their respective employees, other customers, any sponsors, owners and lessees of the premises from all liability, claims, demands, losses or damages as they pertained to a customer's marriage,

122

employment, finances, physical and mental health. I then confirmed that I had heard and understood the United States Department of Health and Human Services STD advisory, authorized ten amero be deducted from the bank account of record for the cover charge, and finally I requested twenty additional amero be transferred from the same account. Twenty Doll Dollars were dispensed from a slot below the screen, and a buzzer sounded letting me know the door was open.

I found an empty table, which wasn't hard to do. Tiny specks of light danced all around, reflecting off a spinning mirror ball suspended from the ceiling. There was an odd collection of people, as usual. Two or three each of rednecks, frat boys and pencil pushers whose wives must've been out of town. A few were clumped together, but most were alone. There was a new girl on stage, a young Latina. A trickle of patrons were making their way to the edge of the stage to slide a Doll Dollar behind her garter.

Once she had finished dancing, the DJ told us to get our dollars ready and welcome to the stage the "sultry Starr". There were a few stray hollers. I didn't yell but I sat up a little straighter in my chair. The next song had started to play but the stage was empty. I didn't recognize the song, but I never did. It sounded okay, though. Starr had good taste. The music pulsed through the speakers as we all waited. One asshole said, "We ain't got all night!"

I knew better. I knew she was coming.

The curtain twitched. Men craned their necks, shifting in their seats to see. Another man yelled, "Where the hell is she?"

The curtain suddenly parted and Starr came out. She strutted down the runway with her head held high, hands on her hips. I watched her through the colored beams of light sweeping the room. She stalked the stage like a caged tigress in stilettos and Cuban heel stockings. The kind with the line up the back. She was built like the 1968 Jaguar XKE in Cale's *Vintage Exotics* calendar. Not the Roadster, but the 2+2 Coupe, the one with the bulge in the hood and the big teardrop-shaped ass-end. Low and fast, all sleek lines and curves, flares and swoops. Starr spun and twirled through the neon glow. Her hips rolled and veered and doubled back, her face flush, hair trailing about her as she spun.

And as always, no one gave much of a shit except me. Even the grey-templed business types, who usually watched the girls with a certain predatory look in their eyes, weren't paying much attention. Maybe it was the fact that Starr was an actual fucking adult, unlike the barely legal runaways at the Silver Fox. Yeah, her tits were losing their battle against gravity, but at least they were real. Maybe it was the little pooch on her belly that made her look like a real woman compared to the 98-pound bimbos down at the Filly's.

From the moment I first saw her, I knew Starr was something different. She had these eyes – a luminous, almost transparent blue, celestial, like the edge of the atmosphere – that just glowed and almost kept me from looking at anything else on her. When she had walked onto that stage on her very first night, I

124

thought back to something I'd learned in 11th grade science, about how if you were to be able to survive a trip into a black hole, as you slipped across the event horizon and plummeted toward the singularity, if you looked back at the universe, time outside would seem to slow to a crawl before finally stopping altogether. That's what happened to me when I first looked at Starr's eyes.

But as hypnotic as her eyes were, as womanly as her body was, on stage her weapon of choice was her ass. If Starr was a battleship, her tits would be the anti-aircraft guns. Those clear blue eyes would be the 38 calibers that could take you down from across the room. But that ass was what sunk you. That ass was the big Mark 7 50-caliber cannon, the one that could swivel all the way around and hit you with a broadside and make you unconditionally surrender.

She had the nicest ass I'd ever seen. Not just at Baby Dolls, but in my whole life. Well, in real life, anyhow. Some of the girls on Cale's *Vintage Exotic Cars* calendar maybe had nicer asses. But that wasn't real life. Starr was real life.

She was short; couldn't have been more than five even. She was wearing fishnet thigh-highs that were too long for her legs. The tops were cutting into her thighs, making her ass look like big scoops of ice cream on a pair of sugar cones. I couldn't decide what flavor.

As I watched her dance, I thought back to how she took me to the VIP room on her first night at work. I don't know if she didn't know the law or didn't care, but she stripped all the way down that night. Her ass looked like Neapolitan, I decided; the vanilla white of her thong tan line, the fresh pink of her cheeks from a recent trip to Lanier's illegal tanning bed, and the seasoned cocoa-tan of her hips and thighs.

"There sure as hell ain't much to you, is there?" I'd said. "But what there is, is finer'n hell."

She had turned 39 not a month earlier, she'd told me. She told me a lot that night she first came to work at Baby Dolls. Maybe too much. First night jitters, maybe. She told me her real name was Cassie, and when I tried to call her that, she said she liked Starr better. She told me about how the day before that 39th birthday her husband, Brayden, a cop, had told her to use his Halo to make dinner reservations anywhere she wanted. Brayden had forgotten about the collection of bikini shots that Sparkle, the 23-year old dispatcher, had sent him.

As she danced, Starr told me how she had promptly dug through the top drawer of her dresser, throwing out bras and panties until she found the garter belt and stockings Brayden gave her for their anniversary the year before. She had stopped grinding her ass in my crotch and demonstrated how she had rolled the stockings onto her legs and licked her finger before touching it to her ass with a "*tsss*". And how she had cried because she looked even fatter in the goddamned thing now than she did last year.

"You ain't fat, darling," I said, and I meant it. "You're just about perfect."

She smiled and said I was crazy, but sweet. Then she told me about how she had looked in mirror and hated her thunder thighs, her big hips and the dimples on her butt. And she told me

126

she had made a promise to herself, right then and there, to not be that woman any longer. She would not ask how fat it made her look. She would stop pointing out that her stockings cut into her thighs. She would stop asking Brayden how he could possibly think she looked good.

Instead, she would be the woman Brayden saw when he looked at her. She would wear the garter belt and the thigh-highs and the thong, even though she couldn't stand the way her ass looked in it. She would have sex with him more than once a month. With the lights on. She would never again give her husband any reason to look at pictures of that skinny whore.

But it had been too late. Brayden had lost his ability to see past the 39 years and the 20 extra pounds. He left her, maybe for his dispatcher, maybe not. Starr didn't know and she didn't care. And she vowed she would make men look at her like that again. She would show Brayden. She would show his scrawny little slut. She answered Lanier's want ad for exotic dancers and took her clothes off and worked the pole the way she'd seen it done in the movies. Lanier said she was too old and too thick, but he knew some of his customers liked that. Lanier told her to come up with a sexier name than Cassie. She already had one in mind.

That was four months ago. Starr had worked six nights a week since and I hadn't missed a single one. After her first dance of this particular night was over I sat and drank for the next few songs, politely declining lap dances from girls that weren't Starr. A continuous stream of girls shook their bodies on stage as I waited. Starr materialized from backstage and began to weave

127

through the empty tables, making her way toward me. Halfway there, a couple of college kids who didn't look old enough to have ordered the beers in their hands, stopped Starr. I saw one boy mouthing something to Starr, probably asking for a dance. Starr shot me a look that seemed to say, *I'll be right there.* Then she smiled at the boys as she slipped off her see-thru nightie and stood in front of them in only her thong and pasties.

I concentrated on Starr as she started dancing, pressing her body between one of the boy's outstretched legs as she moved to the music. I could hear one of the boys say something about Starr being old enough to be his mama. The other boy said, "She's fat enough to be your mama," and the two high-fived.

It took every ounce of willpower I had to stay in my seat and not go over there and jerk a knot in both of them punks' asses. I counted to ten. And Starr wasn't paying them no mind so I tried to let it go.

The boy's hands lit on Starr's back, gliding down onto the swells of her hips. Physical contact between the dancers and the customers was supposed to be against house rules, but Gene, Lanier's Neanderthal of a bouncer, was nowhere to be seen. Neither was Lanier for that matter, not that he would've done anything. Even if Starr complained, Lanier would simply tell her that pissing off the customers was a quick way to lose her tips and possibly her employment. Besides, I'm sure Starr would tell me all the boy was doing was touching her skin. But the second it went beyond that, I was dropping him like a bad transmission.

128

The song ended and Starr pulled the waistband of her thong away from her hip to let the boys slip in a few Doll Dollars. Starr let the elastic snap back against her skin, holding the bill in place. She kissed each boy on the forehead and then walked away, slipping back into her nightie. I watched the boys to make sure they wouldn't mock Starr behind her back. I would have to kick their asses if they did. But all they did was laugh a little bit, which was bullshit but not worth getting in a fight over.

Starr came to my table and sat with me and smiled that smile of hers that could make me forget an awful lot of bullshit.

"Hey," she said. I could see her chest rising, her skin glistening with sweat. I pushed my longneck to her and she took a swig. "Thanks." We sat for a minute and watched Sapphire on stage before Starr stood, taking me by the hand and tugging at me. "Come on."

Starr led me across the floor and through the shimmering curtain that lead to the VIP room. I sunk deep into the couch, the vinyl-clad cushions just about swallowing me up.

Starr kicked at my old boots with her shiny stilettos, letting me know to spread my legs so she could so she could back up between them.

"So," Starr said as she began to grind her ass into my lap. "How was work?"

"Had another dipshit who wanted to argue that her insurance would cover replacing her electrical system if the cops fried it with an EMP."

"I could've told her that." Starr winced at a memory I decided not to ask about.

"I might as well be changing light bulbs or something for a living."

Starr turned to me and sandwiched my face between her breasts. "We're victims of the future, my friend."

I looked up at her from the canyon of her bosom. I could stare at her tits as long as she wasn't talking to me, but I never felt right about looking anywhere but her eyes when she was.

"You should've heard this guy who was in here earlier," she said. "Son of a bitch wouldn't shut up. Of course, he was drunk off his ass. Rich prick, too. He's been in before. Kept talking about all this gasoline he supposedly has stashed somewhere."

"Gasoline?" I asked, my voice muffled.

"Yeah. He was bragging about having a real gas-powered something or other. A boat, maybe. Total perv, too. Yeah, it was a boat, because he kept saying I should come for a ride. Said I should wear a bikini. Said I could go topless and not have to wear these stupid-ass pasties."

"Where's the gas?"

"No idea. Bastard couldn't keep his paws off me. I finally had to call Gene. Lanier was pissed, too."

"I don't blame him."

"No, he was pissed at me."

"Oh."

Starr backed away and danced for a while, cupping her breasts in her palms and then letting her hands roam down her stomach and onto her thighs, around her hips and onto her ass, turning around to let me see. I stared at her body, concentrating on a cluster of freckles on her right ass cheek. It looked like a splatter of ink drops.

"What else did he say?" I asked.

"Jesus, Earlie. You're more interested in him than my ass."

"No, ma'am," I said, eyes on the floor now. "I was just – "

"I'm just fucking with you, sweetie." She turned to face me, still dancing. "Said he was some kind of inspector for the county or some shit. Health inspector, maybe. Hell, I don't know."

I thought about it for a few minutes as I watched Starr's tits. "Might explain why Lanier got mad."

"Damn, I guess it would, huh?"

"Don't explain how he got the gasoline, though."

"Goddammit, Earlie, I ain't kidding now." Starr smashed her tits together and wiggled them at me. "You're starting to give me a complex."

I checked my Halo. "I've got to go anyhow."

Starr dropped her tits and put her hands on her hips. "You do this shit to me every night, you know that, right?"

"When're you going to come with me?" I was extracting myself from the couch.

"You know I don't get off till two, honey."

"It's quarter till."

131

Starr threaded her arms through her nightie. "Lanier would have my ass if he saw me leaving with a customer." She kissed me on the forehead, not unlike she had done to her young admirers. "I will soon, okay? I promise. I want to see who's so important she can pull you away from these." She shook her big tits at me.

I handed her all twenty of my Doll Dollars.

Starr took the bills and stuffed them behind her waistband like a gunslinger holstering a pistol. "I'm starting to get jealous."

"Don't be," I said as I felt around for the split in the curtain. "She ain't even running yet."

***

I held my thumb up to the windshield as I drove to Dugan's, blocking out the mile-long reflective Mylar sheet of the Pepsi logo orbiting the Earth. The space billboard was the size of the full moon in the night sky, but thank the Lord not as bright. If I held my thumb just right, I couldn't even see it.

I tried to find some music like the kind Starr danced to, but I didn't have any feeds that played anything that new. When it all went subscription-based, I'd said fuck it. I'd be damned if I was going to start paying for what I'd been getting free my whole life. With the exception of the stuff at Baby Dolls, I hadn't heard a new song since. Not that I was missing anything. Anyhow, I kept getting interrupted by updates on tomorrow's expected road construction delays and that geomagnetic storm. Maybe it would

132

knock that goddamned Pepsi sign out the sky, I thought. By the time I found a decent song, I had just enough time to listen to the lyrical content advisory before I arrived at Dugan's.

Dugan's was a graveyard. A place of death. Spread out in crooked columns and rows across ten acres of rolling countryside, were tens of thousands of corpses. They lay rotting, their bodies in various states of decomposition, parts broken or wasting away, sometimes missing altogether. There were Fords and Suburus, Cadillacs and BMWs. Makes and models from around the globe, from throughout the past century. Dugan's Salvage was the final resting place for all of them.

I parked the Prius between a couple of recent arrivals that had yet to be taken out back. I pulled my toolbox and an old blanket out of the hatch and took a quick look around. All quiet. I stole to the eight-foot high chain link fence and waited for Baron. After a quick whistle and a rattle of the fence, I heard Baron's tags jingling. The sleek Doberman trotted to the fence, his docked tail wagging as I pulled the pickle pimento loaf from the toolbox, rolling it into a tube. I crouched and tucked the meat through the fence and Baron eagerly snapped it up, saliva oozing from the corners of his mouth.

I stuffed the toolbox under the fence at a place where Baron had tried to dig through and then I unfurled the blanket and lofted it over the barbed wire that capped the chain link. I leapt about halfway up the fence, clambering the rest of the way up and then vaulting myself over, dropping to the dusty ground next to

Baron. I gave the dog a scratch behind the ear and walked into the junkyard.

I made my made through the meandering rows of dead cars. The old steel and iron cars were holding up better than the 21st century cars. The plastic moldings and plastic bumpers and plastic body panels were warped and buckled from exposure to the elements, but the steel, while rusty, still carried itself with defiance and nobility and dignity. The hood ornaments, gleaming winged goddesses and chromed crests, stars and avatars, still bravely pointed the way into promising futures. The fins and vents and swooping chrome bumpers and badges shone in the moonlight, albeit under layers of patina and tangled kudzu.

I skirted the edge of the junkyard and made my way to her, out where the woods closed in. I opened the hood, the hinges groaning, and revealed the 390 cubic-inch V8 engine. It used to be like this, I thought. Laid out before you. Now when you opened a hood, instead of an engine, all you saw were covers, cases and panels. But not a 1963½ Galaxie 500 XL. Not this car.

I hung my work light under the hood and surveyed the engine, reacquainting myself with where I'd left off the last time the sun came up. I had found a Holley 750 on the remains of a mangled '72 Nova about a hundred yards away. It had vacuum secondaries and I wanted mechanical. The float adjustment screw was stripped out, too, but other than that it wasn't in bad shape. I had thought about checking the jets and power valve, but knew I couldn't risk ruining the irreplaceable gaskets. Whatever was in there would have to make do. Last night I had bolted it onto the intake and made the throttle linkage and fuel line connections.

My work was just about done. I tried to count up in my head the nights I'd spent in Dugan's junkyard, bent over the Galaxie's engine, refreshing, refurbishing or rebuilding every part I could, scavenging the other cars to replace the missing or irreparable ones, playing both Dr. Frankenstein and hunchbacked Igor. Nights when my fingers bled without me knowing because my hands were numb from the cold. Nights like tonight when my sweat dripped like a leaky faucet onto valve covers and exhaust headers and shock towers.

I had cherished every minute of it, though. I was grateful for the feel of the steel, the movement of rotating assemblies and the meshing of gears and sprockets. The workings of an engine were predictable, if not reliable. I could look at a spark plug and tell if it was fouled. I could listen to the valves and know if they needed adjustment. I could look at an engine and have a pretty good idea where any trouble was coming from. Electric cars and life in general didn't usually work that way.

I had picked the Galaxie for a lot of reasons. For starters, it was in pretty good condition to begin with. I had even hoped maybe it still ran, but that proved to be a little optimistic. But it wasn't far from it, I knew. Whoever owned it last had clearly loved the car and taken care of it. There was no way to tell how long it had been sitting at Dugan's. I guessed twenty years, but maybe not even that long. Only two of the tires had gone flat but they'd held a steady 35 psi since I snuck them into Cale's and pumped them up. The fabric of the upholstery had barely begun to deteriorate, and only in the spots the sun hit every day. She didn't even smell musty inside, which told me she didn't let in the rain.

She was parked in the farthest corner of Dugan's, which meant I could work far from the road. She was straight and solid and didn't have too much rust. And there were plenty of other cars in Dugan's yard that had interchangeable parts. Organ donors, I thought of them. But most importantly, Starr would love her. She had mentioned once that she loved Galaxies. I knew that Starr loved the things in the night sky, and she could have easily been talking about actual galaxies. But I liked the idea of that beautiful creature having a thing for old Fords. So that's what I told myself.

I had no idea what I would do with the car when I got it running. Maybe I'd just sneak out to Dugan's every now and then and cruise the dirt aisles amongst the derelict automobiles, like some kind of ghost wandering a cemetery. Maybe I'd crash through the gate and go tear-assing through the countryside until the cops caught me. Or maybe I'd just strip it all down and do it again, to stay in practice. I didn't know. But I promised myself one thing: one day I would see Starr in that Galaxie.

There were about four hours of darkness left and I spent every minute of them getting the cooling system ready. Radiator from a 1981 Ford LTD, water pump from a '66 Fairlane, aluminum flex fan from a '75 Blazer, new belts and hoses, overflow catch can made from a Pabst Blue Ribbon tallboy. I had left myself with only one more task; wiring the distributor. For a minute I thought about combing the junkyard again for a

136

distributor cap that would fit and wasn't cracked, but I knew if I hadn't found one by now, it wasn't here. Anyhow, my package from Cristóbal should come in any day and then I'd be all set.

I worked on the car until the sky in the east turned a pale amber. I wondered what that sunrise would look like over the Atlantic Ocean. And in my mind I put Starr on that big Snap-On screwdriver where Miss August had been sitting, paddling across the sea.

I shut the Galaxie's hood and winked at the Virgin Mary on the air freshener dangling from the rearview. I thanked her for another night of watching over me. I didn't believe in her or her kid, but I knew my nightly work in Dugan's junkyard was doing for my soul what Mary's young'un did for some others folks'.

The sun was rising and Dugan would be showing up soon, and I needed to be at Cale's in an hour. I had just enough time to run home, shower, put on my uniform and punch in at 7:30.

***

My Halo started chirping at midnight and didn't quit until 12:04 when I finally sat upright on the couch. My back hurt even worse than normal. After all night doubled over the Galaxie, I had spent the following day in a fetal position under the dash of one of those old hydrogen Lexuses. A man wearing capri pants and a visor had brought it in. Its reactive cup holder temperature system had shit the bed, leaving the driver with a vehicle that didn't automatically maintain its owner's beverage of choice. The diagnostics computer had initially indicated a faulty ground. It had taken most of the day but I had finally tracked the problem to a leak in the refrigerant line that supplied the cooling side of the system.

"Thank the Lord," I had said to Miss August as I put away my tools at the end of the day. "That dude almost had to sip a lukewarm grande mocha whatever-the-fuck-they're-called."

Now it was time to go see Starr again. As I stood from the couch, my Halo told me to expect light to moderate lower back that night.

"No shit."

The Halo recommended seeking the advice of a physician if my discomfort persisted.

"Fuck off."

I shuffled to my front door, ignoring the Halo as it told me my weight and body mass index and precisely what percentage of each I'd need to reduce in order to comply with federal well-being guidelines. I opened my front door, the air like a hot, wet blanket, and saw on my stoop and small cardboard box.

"Thank you, Cristóbal," I said as I sealed out the muggy night again.

I tore into the box, pulling out something roughly the size of my fist, wrapped in crumpled brown paper. I snatched off the wrapping and looked at my shiny new distributor cap. I flipped it over, examined the inside. It looked okay except for the *Hecho en Cuba* molded into the plastic. No way to tell if it would work till I tried it, but the same could be said for most of the parts on the

138

Galaxie. I hated the thought of foreign junk on her, but it was my only real option. It was all foreign junk even back when I could legally buy internal combustion parts in the States, anyways.

I spoke to my Halo. "Cristóbal."

"Bueno," a voice came back a few seconds later.

I'd never met Cristóbal Gomez. Cristóbal had first contacted me after I had asked about his "Michigan Movies". When the Helms Tax went into effect, it effectively tripled the cost of porn files as well as instituted fines for unregistered files, putting the cost of viewing pornography out of reach of the common man. Which was the whole idea. The pornography lobbyists had kept smut from being outlawed, but maybe it would've been better had they lost. Just like they'd done with cigarettes, alcohol and marijuana, what the government couldn't ban they taxed to death. It would've been easier to find XXX videos had they been simply illegal instead of priced out of reach. But just like Prohibition and the pre-legalization days of weed, you can get a hold of just about anything if you know who and how to ask. So a network of sellers arose with a novel way to distribute smut away from the watchful eye of the Man: digital video discs. Any files on a Halo or any other Blink-based device were obviously going to show up on the federal grid. But anyone with an old-fashioned DVD player could buy their porn on a physical disc and watch it without the government ever knowing.

I had discovered the underground porn railroad on accident. I wasn't even looking for porn, not that I have any kind of moral objections to it or anything. But I had been scouring the internet for footage of Ford's old factory in Dearborn, Michigan. I just wanted to see how they built them back then. I followed a link that said, "thousands of Michigan movies for home delivery." I gave them my Halo address and said I'd like to know more. In about five minutes I got a call from a man named Cristóbal. I just about couldn't understand him with his accent but I finally figured out that Cristóbal wanted to know exactly what kind of movies I was interested in. When I told him I was looking for footage of the assembly line at the Dearborn factory, Cristóbal started acting funny.

"Assembly line?" he asked.

"Yeah. The 1950's if you got it, but anything really would be alright."

"I am not familiar with 'assembly line'," Cristóbal had said. "Is that like a gang bang?"

The conversation that ensued was rife with misunderstandings and repeated queries. Cristóbal and I gradually realized that we were speaking completely different languages, and I don't mean English and Spanish. I was asking if this man had any videos of old Fords being put together. Cristóbal was speaking in the vernacular of the distributor of illicit goods. Everything was a euphemism, in the likely event he and his potential customer were being eavesdropped on. It took a couple of return calls and some pretty serious anti-Uncle Sam rhetoric, but I finally convinced Cristóbal that I wasn't with the FBI. Cristóbal eventually explained to me that he was, in his own words, an importer and exporter. "An acquirer of commodities", he said. Things no longer readily available in the United States, he said, "readily available" in this case meaning "illegal". Cristóbal told me that when someone wants "Michigan movies", they're usually talking about skin flicks.

"*Mee*shigan, you see, is shaped like your right hand, no?"

I had looked at my right hand and agreed, assuming I was wearing an oven mitt.

"And most people use their right hand when they're watching a porno, yes?"

I got it. I quickly learned that if I wanted cigarettes, I needed to ask about 'funeral arrangements' (cigarettes, aka "coffin nails"). If I was looking for a prostitute, for example, I should ask about a 'deep sea fishing trip' ("hookers"). None of it fooled the Feds, Cristóbal said, but a good lawyer could work with it.

"What if I'm looking for parts for an internal combustion engine?" I had asked.

The question had been answered initially with silence. Then, "What do you need?" A challenge had been accepted.

"Dinosaur bones" became our term for auto parts. Over the next few months, Cristóbal had come through time and again with parts that I couldn't fix or find at Dugan's. Fuel pump, oil pressure sending unit, fresh belts and hoses, headlights. The only thing Cristóbal hadn't been able to deliver was the gaskets for the carburetor, and he had actually found those only to have them have them get lost in the mail.

I knew I couldn't have gotten this close to starting that engine without Cristóbal's help. I supposed I'd even call the guy a friend, as much as you can be friends with someone you'd never met. He knew about Starr. I knew he had a wife and a little boy in Havana, and as soon as he made enough money he was going back there to stay. Take them to Varadero. Or Cayo Coco, maybe.

I also knew he had a couple of boats; the *Siluro* (which meant 'catfish', he told me), a small, wooden flat bottom deal he used to ferry goods up and down the river; and the *Mantarraya*, or Stingray, a go-fast boat not unlike the ones they raced offshore, I imagined. He stuck to the rivers because the roads were too well controlled. Check points, toll booths, cameras, satellite surveillance. He used the Mantarraya to make the transit from undisclosed locations along the Southern coast of the U.S. down to Cuba.

"Hey, listen man," I said to my Halo. "Thanks."

"Glad to help. Think it's going to work?"

"It should." I turned the distributor cap over in my hand. "It looks fine. I really appreciate it."

"Absolutely, partner," Cristóbal said. "Anything else?"

"Oh, hey, I don't know the word for it, but it's the stuff that…you know…" I was trying to tell Cristóbal about the gasoline Starr had mentioned.

"No, I don't know."

"You don't want to make any *funeral arrangements* around it."

"Que?"

142

"Dinosaur juice."

"Si! You need some, man?" Cristóbal said.

"No, actually I might have some for sell. You buying?"

"Always buying."

"I'll keep you posted," I said and hung up.

I grabbed a slice of pickle pimento loaf and headed out.

***

Starr-Time, as she liked to call it, always began without Starr. She told me she'd asked the DJ more than once to introduce her like that: "Are you ready for Starr-Time?" He told Starr he didn't shake his hairy ass in a g-string so she shouldn't try to be a DJ. I guess he had a point.

The DJ told the crowd to put our hands together and get those Doll Dollars ready for the "seductive Starr". Starr liked to give her song a minute to build up before she took the stage. There was some random applause and an errant whoop. The stage slowly disappeared behind the veil produced by the smoke machine. The vapor looked like it was glowing when the purple spotlights would sweep through, searching for any signs of Baby Doll's next performer.

Starr was waiting. She understood what this was all about. She was virgin sacrifice and King Kong rolled into one. I think I was the only person in this room other than Starr who got it.

She burst onto the stage, prancing and posing, stopping here and there to sling her hair around like a lasso. Her eyes were tired, I could tell. She was wearing too much mascara. Her outfit was a little too tight in all the wrong places. She'd forgotten to spit her gum out. She was perfect.

I had given each of Starr's moves a different name in my head, all named after great cars Detroit didn't have the balls to build anymore. At the start of every dance, when she shot through the backstage curtains and strutted down the runway, hands on her hips, spike heels hitting the stage in perfect time to the beat— I called that the Charger. When she'd sink to her knees and crawl away, her ass stuck high in the air and twitching like a mischievous cat's tail, that was the Cougar. Then there was the Stingray, where Starr would slowly cruise to edge of the stage, pacing menacingly toward me, hips swinging deliberately. She would step closer until it seemed as if she might march right onto my chest before turning away, like an effortlessly swimming manta ray veering away from a diver at the last second. There was also the Cyclone (bending straight over at the waist and swirling her hips in fast, tiny circles), the Firebird, (rolling onto her back and grabbing her ankles, spreading her legs like wings, giving everyone an unobstructed view of her crotch), and the Thunderbolt (crashing to her knees at the base of the chrome pole and then touching the tip of her tongue to it, licking it all the way up as she stood to full height). Regardless of their name, all of those moves had one thing common: there was an invisible wire strung from Starr's ass to my hard-on, and every time her ass moved my cock jerked and bounced with it.

Her ass seemed to dance on its own. It was electric. An entire fleet of Prii could be cranked with less current. Her hands loved her ass. I couldn't blame them. Her hands would sometimes comb through her long hair or cup her breasts when she was on stage, but their favorite place to be was on that ass.

She fell to her knees, bucking up and down, a tidal wave of lust and anger and adrenaline channeled into her moves, blissfully oblivious to the apathy of the crowd. There were less than a dozen paying customers tonight, and only two of us were eyeing Starr with any interest at all.

I split time between watching Starr and watching the other man who was watching her. He looked rich, like he'd have the money to keep Starr in the VIP room all night if he wanted to. And I could tell by the way he was looking at her, he wanted to. If I was going to get any private time with Starr tonight, I'd have to catch her before the other guy did. When we made eye contact, I gave him my steeliest glare.

Then the irony of it hit me, that I got pissed off when these dipshits didn't pay any attention to Star, then I got mad when they paid too much. I thought about how it would probably make Starr's night if this rich guy asked her for a dance in the back. So maybe I should just sit here peacefully and let it all unfold. But then I decided that I didn't want to do that after all.

No sooner was I thinking all that than I saw the guy walk to the stage. Starr was on her knees, wrapping her fingers around the runway's pole and touching the tip of her tongue to it as she stared down her waiting admirer. She stood, running her tongue up the metal pole like it was a chrome candy cane. She reached behind her, untied her bikini top and let if fall away, showing her naked tits to everyone. Her nipples, of course, were hidden safely behind neon yellow pasties that glowed like a pair of headlights under the club's black lights.

The man had a stack of Doll Dollars out and ready, folding one lengthwise as he smiled up at Starr. She tugged at her gold hot pants and stepped closer to the edge of the stage. The man's hands were suddenly all over her, pulling at her stockings, grabbing her thighs, squeezing her ass. I bolted out of my seat, ready to tackle the guy and administer a black eye or two if I had time before Gene jumped on me. But Starr quickly stepped back, just out of arm's reach. She was still dancing, still smiling. Of course Gene was nowhere to be seen. I watched her for a second. If anything she seemed flattered, not threatened, by the extra attention. *She's fine*, I told myself. *Sit your dumb ass down.*

I took my seat and watched as Starr shimmied her hot pants over her hips and down around her ankles. She stepped out of them and kicked them toward her eager friend. Starr was naked now except for her pasties, thigh-highs and heels, and a little thong with sequins all over it.

Starr walked to the edge of the stage, turned to one side and pulled the waistband of her thong away, letting the guy arrange a half dozen dollars along her hip. He immediately held up another fan of bills, showing them to Starr, and she turned and let him put those on her other hip.

I watched his hands. My daddy always said you could tell a lot about a man from his hands. Mine were ugly, gnarled things that looked like knotty wood. This guy's were smooth, like the hardest work they'd ever done was sign his name. Hell, they were almost shiny. Come to think of it, this guy's hands looked a lot like Brayden Podner's.

And the son of a bitch held up more dollars, and Starr giggled and turned her back to him and pulled the thong from the split of her ass like she was drawing back a slingshot. As soon as he stuffed the rest of his bills in there he was grabbing her ass again. He tried to pull down her panties but Starr held them tight in both hands. I jumped up again, ready to beat some rich boy ass, but Starr got away and shot me a look that told me to calm the fuck down. She took a deep breath and turned and walked back down the runway, her jiggling ass garnished with a fringe of Doll Dollars. She disappeared behind the curtain just as the song ended.

Diamond was next onstage but my eyes were glued to the backstage entrance. Halfway through Diamond's song, Starr came out in her nightie and headed in my direction. She didn't get far. Lanier's fat ass stepped from shadows and blocked Starr's path. His bald dome reflected the club's lights like a disco ball. Gene was at his side, dwarfing his boss, who wasn't a whole lot taller than Starr. Gene's arms were folded, making them look even bigger. I watched, trying to tell from Starr's reactions what they were saying to her. Surely they were getting Starr's side of the story before showing Rich Boy the door. I eyed him and laughed to myself. I wondered if he knew he was about to get thrown out on his ass.

Rich Boy stood and wobbled to the trio that was discussing his fate. He was a little drunker than I realized. Lanier turned to welcome the man into the conversation, going so far as to put his arm around him. I could hear Lanier's booming voice, just one of many manifestations of his Napoleon complex, as he thanked the customer for coming out tonight. I had seen this before. *We're giving you the boot, but we'd like for to you return and spend your money with us again at a later, less obnoxious date.* After a big slap on the back and one of Lanier's patented used car salesman smiles, he and Gene slipped back into the shadows. And then Starr took the customer by the hand and led him away to the VIP room.

I shouldn't have been surprised. I should've known that no way in hell was Lanier going to kick out a guy with perfectly good cash. I watched Starr and the man until they were out of view. I wanted to go back there and drag that guy out by his comb-over. I wanted to crash into Lanier's office and punch him in his chins until he understood what it meant to respect a lady. More than anything, I wanted to take Starr away from both of them. But I didn't do any of those things. Instead I sat and waited.

The minutes began to pile up. My mind raced. *What if he's touching her?* I thought. *What if she's letting him? What if Lanier is making her?* Five minutes went by. Then five more. I tried not to imagine what was happening behind that sparkly curtain. Then, because I couldn't help it, I would picture just that. Was she on

148

her knees between his legs, ass sticking out behind her, arms draped across his thighs as she lashed her hair against his crotch, like she always did with me? Was she whispering to him how she liked his hands. Were those blue eyes glittering up at him?

I waited through three songs before I got up and walked back to the VIP room, barging through the curtain. I'm not sure what I thought I'd see. What I did see was Rich Boy sunk back into the couch, Starr writhing in his lap. Rich Boy's hands were clamped onto Starr's ass, his fingers digging into her soft flesh. He was watching me, peeking around Starr's hip, a shit-eating grin on his face.

I started counting to ten. I got to three.

I pushed past Starr and pulled the guy up by his collar.

"Time's up, Hoss. I'm cutting in." I slung him toward the door, his lack of balance making it easy. He made like he was going to come back after me and Starr stepped out of the way. I hit my best *bring it on* pose, ready to tag his drunk ass. He stared at me for a minute, called me a motherfucker and something else that was too slurred to make out, then walked away.

"What the fuck did you do that for, Earlie?" Starr said.

"He was grabbing your ass!"

"I'm a stripper. Sometimes guys grab my ass. Occupational hazard." She stared at me for a couple of seconds. "Jesus, you just cost me at least fifty amero."

I didn't know what to say. So I didn't say anything.

"I don't need protecting, Earlie," she said. She was wrong. Or at least I wanted her to be.

"Sorry." I turned to walk out.

"Wait. Listen," she said. "I'm sorry. That was sweet, what you did. I should be thanking you, not yelling at you. Come here."

Starr pulled me by the hand and I plopped down on the couch. She began to dance for me.

"You owe me fifty amero, though," she said. "And you know Gene will be back here any minute to beat the shit out of you."

"I ain't scared of Gene."

"Yeah, well, maybe you ought to be."

Gene was bigger than hell, but he was dumb. And I wasn't scared, that wasn't just talking shit.

"So, before I was so rudely," Starr said. "I found out more about that gasoline I was telling you about."

"From who?"

"From the guy you just threw out of here, genius."

"That was the guy?"

"Yeah, that was the guy."

"Shit."

"Yeah."

Starr danced for a few minutes and I watched. There were seven of those freckles on her right ass cheek. Another song came on.

"So, what did he say?" I finally asked.

"You want the good news or the bad news?"

"Do I have a choice?"

"The bad news is that he's the county health inspector."

"Woops."

"Yeah, no shit. That's why Lanier made me bring him here."

"Fuck, I'm sorry," I said.

"Nothing we can do about it now."

I watched the curtain, waiting for Gene's giant ass to come busting through any second now.

"So what's the good news?"

"I know where the gasoline is," Starr said.

"Yeah?"

"Oh yeah. He's got a buddy that's a cop. And this cop found a couple hundred gallons of gas when he raided a house that was growing tobacco."

"Convenient."

"Yeah. So, this cop calls up our inspector and tells him he'll split the street value of the gas with him if he can find a place to store it for a few days."

"He told you all this?"

"Yeah. I think he thought I would be impressed. Plus he's drunker than shit," Starr said. "And I'm not without a certain charm."

"What's that mean?"

Starr smiled. "I might have led him to pussy and then told him he couldn't drink."

"You showed him your pussy?"

"Now that would be against the rules, wouldn't it?"

I realized this prick had seen Starr's pussy and I hadn't. And apparently it was written all over my face.

"Hey," Starr said. "You want to know where that gasoline is, don't you?"

In my head I could see perfectly that son of bitch's hands white-knuckling Starr's pretty ass. I pushed it away as hard as I could. "Yeah. Yeah, I guess I do."

"Well, I know."

"Where is it?"

"He said it was at some apartment complex," Starr said.

"In tanks, or what?"

"He didn't say. All he said was that he had condemned one of the buildings. Somewhere off Myers Road. Know it?"

"I know Myers Road, yeah. Trying to think of an apartment complex out there..."

Starr had stopped dancing at some point. She was just standing there, wearing next to nothing, looking at me. "Hey, listen," she said. "Sorry I bitched at you."

"I had it coming."

She smiled at me. "That was actually pretty hot, that you came in here to save me."

"I didn't save nobody."

"Yeah, you did." She leaned over and kissed me on the lips.

She was so fucking pretty. Her hips swung and spiraled, her arms coiling above her head like wisps of smoke. She cupped her breasts in her hands and plucked at each pasty until they

152

started to peel away. She pulled them off like band-aids, her nipples stretching and then snapping back when they were freed. She turned, watching me over her shoulder as she began to roll down her thong with the heels of her palms. When she had it around her thighs, she grabbed her ankles.

She said, "You know it doesn't get much more naked than knowing somebody's looking at your asshole."

"Well, it's a real nice – "

I was interrupted by a sound like the ones Baron used to make before I learned the pickle pimento loaf trick. I peered around Starr to see Gene swatting the curtain out of his way as he stomped into the VIP room. Starr scrambled to pull her panties up while at the same time trying to block Gene's path to me. He swatted her away, too. He stood over me like some kind of super-villain or something, waiting for me to get up so he could throw me around.

I thought about kicking him the balls, and even though that might have bought me the couple of seconds I'd need to dash past him, kicking somebody in the balls is pretty low, even if it's a big-ass bouncer who's about to knock the shit out of you. Besides, that would have meant running out on Starr, and I'd take two ass-kickings from Gene if it got Starr to leave this place with me.

As I was thinking all that, it dawned on me that it wasn't necessarily a foregone conclusion that Gene could whip me. Yeah, he was about a foot taller and had probably fifty pounds on me. And his arms were as big around as my legs. But it's like Big Earl used to say, it ain't the size of the –

About that time, Gene slapped his hands over my shoulders and snatched me off the couch. He sent me head first through the air, my left shoulder hitting the floor and skidding until I came to rest sprawled out at Lanier's shoes. My Doll Dollars flipped and fluttered to the carpet all around me. Starr screamed, like only a scared woman can, and ran to me, only to get yanked back by Gene. He held her in place with a big hand clamped on the back of her neck.

"Put your clothes on, you whore," Lanier said, like he was spitting out something that had gone bad.

I scrambled to my feet and threw a haymaker right at Lanier's fat neck, only to have it hooked away by Gene's arm.

"Bad idea, dude," Gene said. He spun me around like a top and the last thing I saw before everything went black was a sledgehammer that looked an awful lot like Gene's clenched fist.

A vertical sea of gravel swam into focus and I realized I was lying in the parking lot. I could hear Starr yelling at somebody to go fuck themselves and the then sound of a door slamming. Then I felt her hair on my face and then her hands on my shoulders.

"You okay?" Her voice sounded distant.

My bottom lip was split open and I could feel a trickle running from the corner of my mouth. Starr helped me to my feet. I staggered backwards but didn't fall.

My Halo said, "You have potentially suffered a mild concussion. Please seek immediate medical assistance."

"Where's that son of a bitch at?" I slurred through jangly teeth. I moved toward the door of the club only to have Starr stand in the way.

"You're not going back in there," she said.

"Why not?"

"One, because Gene might just kill you. And two, because they just called the sheriff's department and the last person in the world I want to see right now is my ex-husband."

I looked at her. She was still in her thong, thigh-highs, heels and nothing else. I took off my t-shirt and gave it to Starr. It came halfway down her thighs, leaving a sliver of white skin between the smoky lace tops of her stockings and the dingy hem of my shirt. She held onto me as we walked across the parking lot, teetering in her high heels, until we got to my Prius.

For the next couple of minutes the mean-ass woman who talked to me from my dash gave me the usual bullshit about national security and waivers and disclaimers, only now they were amended to include liability issues related to a passenger.

I tried not to stare. Somehow Starr looked even sexier in my old t-shirt than she did with no clothes on. I could feel her looking at me, shirtless. I tried to suck in my gut without making it obvious, but no matter what I did I couldn't keep my jeans from cutting into my belly and making a roll that hung over my belt. I wanted to explain to her that I wasn't really that fat, it was just how I was sitting, but I figured she knew that already.

My car told me, "Your passenger lives at 1000, Apartment 6, Blue Ridge Court."

"Don't take me there," Starr said quickly.

For a long time neither one of us said anything else, we just rode, my goddamned car asking every five minutes where I was going and if I needed directions.

Finally I said, "I'm sorry about what happened back there."

"Don't be. I hated that job anyhow."

"You told me you liked it."

"I liked..." Starr stopped, like she was making sure to say the right thing. Then she decided not to say anything. She reclined the seat back as far as it would go and hung her feet out the open window. I watched as she used the stiletto heel of one shoe to push the other off her foot until it suddenly vanished, caught by the wind, gone into the night. She kicked the other shoe off into the blackness to share its match's fate. "Won't be needing those anymore." She rolled down each stocking until they clung only to her toes, the nylon streaming from her feet, whipping like pennants from the masts of a tall ship. Finally the wind took each of those as well.

The Prius asked again if I needed directions.

"Shut up, you jabbering bitch," I pounded my fist on the dash. The car's voice didn't miss a beat, telling me I had travelled seventeen miles with no apparent destination. It asked me if this trip was really necessary and then informed me that needless travel strained our nation's infrastructure.

156

Suddenly my Halo began talking, too. "You have lost approximately 200 milliliters of blood." I had forgotten about my busted lip. "If you need medical assistance, please – "

"Damn it, you too?" I unsnapped my Halo from my wrist and threw it in the backseat.

It wouldn't be quiet. "Please be advised that unauthorized removal of your Halo is a misdemeanor punishable by law."

"Jesus Christ," I said. Starr was trying not to laugh.

"Please reaffix your Halo within thirty seconds to avoid having local law enforcement and rescue officials notified of its removal. Thirty, twenty-nine, twenty-eight…"

Starr was giggling. We listened to my Halo do its self-destruct impersonation.

"…twenty-two, twenty-one…"

"Fuck you!" I yelled at the bracelet in the backseat.

"Just put it back on, Earlie," Starr said. "I don't really feel like talking to the police. Not after the night we've had."

"Nope. No way. I'm making a stand."

"…eleven, ten, nine…"

"Come on, Earlie. This ain't funny no more."

"I ain't doing it."

"…four, three…"

I waited as long as I thought I could then reached back and grabbed the damned thing. I slapped it around my wrist just as the countdown hit zero.

"What a rebel," Starr said. She watched me with those stratosphere-blue eyes for a half a mile.

I pulled onto the shoulder of the road and shut the car off.

"Get in the back," I said.

Without a word, Starr climbed into what passed for a backseat in my Prius. It was about half the size of the couch in the VIP room. She pulled off the t-shirt and then did a contortionist's act until she had wrestled her spangled thong down to her ankles. I tugged it the rest of the way off and crammed myself into the backseat with her, unbuckling, unbuttoning and unzipping along the way.

In a heartbeat I was on her, locking limbs, pinning wrists. Mounting, saliva and fingers. I snarled. Starr gasped. There was a flurry of motion, flashes of pale skin. Clenched fists, gurgled moans, muscles tensing and letting go. But I couldn't get inside her.

Starr was looking over her shoulder, watching me with eyes like slits. "Fuck me," she hissed.

"I'm trying!"

Starr bowed back against me, pressing me against the ceiling of the car. She spread her legs, reached back between them to guide me in. I used the ceiling like a fulcrum to get some leverage, but I couldn't get the angle. I pushed my body against hers until she lost the strength in her arms and slipped into the floor. She felt for the door handle and grabbed it, bracing herself against it. My hands moved around her waist and up her soft belly, cupping her breasts, squeezing tightly; back down her arched spine, onto her ass, grabbing handfuls of it and kneading.

But I still couldn't get inside her. There just wasn't enough room in the car.

"Dammit!" I said before collapsing onto the seat back, my hard-on pointing uselessly at Starr.

I jumped when the bitch in the dash started talking again. "Please be advised loitering is prohibited in this area. Please continue to your destination or request roadside assistance."

"Man, fuck this car." I said. I kicked and crawled my way back into the front seat, zipping up once I was back behind the wheel. Starr was fighting her way back into my t-shirt. "I got a plan."

Fifteen minutes later we pulled up to the gate at Dugan's.

"Yuck," Starr said as I peeled the pickle pimento loaf slice off my 9/16" wrench. "Please tell me you're not going to eat that."

I let her worry for a few seconds until Baron came trotting up to the fence to slurp up the lunchmeat. I hurled the blanket over the barbed wire then cradled Starr's barefoot in my hand before clean-and-jerking her most of the way up the fence. Despite the fact that I'd just tried to stick my dick in her, I didn't look up her shirt when she went over the top. I vaulted over and took her hand as we walked into the junkyard.

I led her past the rows of abandoned cars, with their battered grills and shattered windshields, until we got to the Galaxie.

"Well, here she is," I said.

Starr looked over the car. "So this is what you leave me for every night." She trailed her fingertips down the Galaxie's curved fender. "She's beautiful."

I pulled on the driver's side door, its hinges giving way with a tortured groan. I gently flipped up the seat, spread the blanket out and ushered Starr into the Galaxie's cavernous back bench. She smiled and took my hand as I helped her in. There was enough room back there for her to stretch out. I climbed in after her, the ancient springs in the seat creaking and pinging under my weight. She unbuckled my belt and popped open the button of my jeans, snaking her hand inside and squeezing the hard-on that hadn't gone away since we'd pulled over in the Prius. She cupped the nape of my neck in her palm and pulled my open mouth to hers.

She tugged the t-shirt up and over her breasts and watched me as I looked at her body. My vintage exotic. Smiling at me, she lazily rolled onto her stomach. I waited, admiring, my eyes roaming over her shape. She spread her legs, showed me more. I gazed at her, her thighs, the split of her ass, the dimple of her asshole looking like it had been made with the poke of a finger; looking for all the world like it was beckoning me to come and do something unintended to it.

The need to touch her overwhelmed me and I laid my hands on her ass. She pushed it into my palms and I clutched and kneaded it. She tightened the halves into clenched bunches and then let them relax into full, soft globes for me to squeeze.

"I love your ass."

160

"I know."

"I've always loved your ass."

"I know, Earlie."

"You've got the—"

"Why don't you shut up about it and fuck it?"

Her smile was gone, replaced by something intense and needy. I lowered my body onto hers, my mouth searching in her hair for her ears and neck. Her legs were spread out below me and she arched her back like a hunter's bow being drawn tight.

"Do it," she said. And I did.

I pushed into her, pressing her body against the brittle vinyl of the backseat. Her perfume and the smells of the old car quickly gave way to other scents. I held her by her hips, my fingers digging into the soft flesh there. Starr watched me over her shoulder, eyes flashing in the dark. She groaned at the fullness. We fucked like first-timers— awkwardly, sometimes hesitantly, but with unashamed want, filling the interior of the car with growled demands and gasped promises.

I tried to maintain control of myself, tried to think of something, anything, to keep it from ending. I tried to think about the Galaxie. I thought about piston rings and main bearings and valve seals, but it all evaporated like droplets of water on a hot intake manifold. My body shuddered and I went light-headed. Behind clenched eyelids I saw nebulae and supernovae exploding.

For a long time afterwards, with the exceptions of our heaving chests, we were still, holding each other in the backseat, looking up through the Galaxie's back glass at the black sky.

Then I would gaze down at Starr's body, finding myself again considering the seven ink spot freckles on her ass. I ran my hand across her skin where they were.

"You like them, don't you?" she said.

"I do."

"It's Cassiopeia."

"Who?"

"Cassiopeia. It's a constellation."

"I thought they were freckles," I said.

"It's a tattoo." She propped herself up on her elbow and looked over her shoulder at her ass, as if making sure she remembered the design correctly. "She's who I'm named after. She was the wife of King Cepheus. She bragged about her beauty and Poseidon punished her by destroying their kingdom." She looked up through the glass for a couple of seconds then pointed. "There they are."

I looked through the dusty glass and saw nothing.

"Come here," she said, climbing out of the car to stand naked in the junkyard. I came out behind her and aimed my line of sight down her outstretched arm. "There."

It didn't look like any queen I'd ever seen, but I nodded and said, "Oh, okay."

"After they died, Cassiopeia and Cepheus were placed among the stars by Poseidon. Cassiopeia is upside-down half the year because of her vanity."

I gazed at Cassiopeia for a few seconds then gazed at Starr. Starr was so much prettier.

162

***

The time clock at Cale's acquired my Halo at 7:38am. My hands got to work replacing a self-parking sensor in the front bumper of something, but my brain was stuck on Starr.

She had lied in my arms on the hood of the Galaxie, her head on my bare chest as she pointed out constellations and told me their stories until the sky in the east began to glow. It had been even better than working on the car. I drove her back to Baby Dolls as the sun came up and she got in her car and drove away. Every moment since, images of her have flashed through my head like the glossy pages of a Snap-On calendar. *February:* Starr on a heart-shaped bed, legs wrapped around a giant ratchet and socket. *July:* Dressed as the Statue of Liberty, a stiff breeze blowing up her dress to reveal a garter belt, raising a pair of vise grips wrench instead of a torch. *October:* In a skintight devil costume, complete with horns and pointy tail, holding a pitchfork in one hand, impact wrench in the other. *December:* Starr as Santa's helper in a fur-trimmed red suit, breasts spilling out, a sack full of chromed hand tools for good little mechanics.

"Earl!" Brayden Podner's voice intruded upon my bliss. "I need to see you in my office."

He was behind a tiny desk in what used to be the supplies closet when Cale ran things.

"What can I do for you, Mr. Podner?"

He was looking at his Halo. "Well, for starters, I see here that you were eight minutes late this morning."

"That's right," I said, refusing to apologize. My tardiness had been worth every second.

"Of course the eight minutes will be docked from your pay."

"Of course."

"How many days has it been since a razor touched your face, Earl?"

The more he talked, the more I regretted not calling in sick. My Halo would have even backed me up. I did have a mild concussion, after all.

"I've a good mind to send you home and have you press that uniform, too."

I could be with Starr right now, I thought. We could be in her bed, tangled in her sheets.

"You know, Podner, that's a wonderful idea. I think I will go press my uniform." And with that, I walked out of the supplies closet and went to my tool box. I closed the lid and began pushing the cabinet through the garage, past the door to the sales office, where Brayden stood mouthing something I was unable to hear over the deafening rattle of the hundreds of tools vibrating and bouncing inside.

"Can't hear you, Podner!" I yelled as I pushed my tool chest by him and out an open roll-up door to the Prius. As I was opening the hatch, Cale walked up and grabbed one of the handles on the tool chest and helped me hoist it into the car. The whole
164

back end of the car squatted under the weight. The hatch wouldn't close so I had to leave it pointing skyward.

"Thanks, buddy," I said, shaking Cale's calloused hand. "I hate to leave you hanging."

"My pension kicks in on January One," my old boss said with a wink. "You take care of yourself. Come to see me sometime. Edith's all the time asking about you."

"I just might do that," I said, knowing it was bullshit. I could tell by his smile he knew it, too. I got in my car and drove off, my middle finger hung out the window and aimed at the Current logo above the door.

Every minute or so the Prius would remind me that its hatch was open. The events of the last twelve hours ran in a loop in my head. How it had all started with Rich Boy's hands on Starr's sweet ass. How if that had never happened, I would have never thrown him out of the VIP room, and had I never done that, Starr probably would've never pulled her panties down for me. Lanier would've never fucked with us, and I would've never swung at him. And Gene wouldn't have had to knock me out. As bad as that part sucked, if not for that, Starr wouldn't have been with me when I came to. We wouldn't have gone for a ride in my shitbox Prius. And if my car wasn't such a little piece of crap, I might not have had the idea to take her to see the Galaxie. She would've never shown me the Seven Sisters and I would've gotten to work on time and not caught hell from Brayden. Which means I would've never quit my job and driven to Starr's house at nine o'clock in the morning, trying to remember just whose fault all this was.

Rich Boy. It was all his fault. The good parts and the bad. Him and his contraband gasoline.

I spoke to my Halo. "Cristóbal"

"Bueno," he said a couple of seconds later.

"Remember that dinosaur juice I mentioned?"

"Man, have I got some good shit." He hadn't heard a word I said. "You want some?"

"No, I'm good. Listen, I –"

"I ain't talking about marijuana, man. I'm talking about *funeral arrangements*." I could hear Cristóbal take a long drag off a cigarette, then fight off a cough that finally broke out with a sound like laughing hyena. "I even like the coughing, man. It reminds me of the good old days. Back when tobacco was the villain." He wasn't making much sense, but I let him keep talking. "There is a continuous tug-of-war going on in America, mi amigo. Between heroes and villains. And whichever side is winning, they're called the villains. When the heroes start winning again, then they become the villains."

"I have no idea what you're talking about, Cristóbal."

"Cristóbal Colón, man! The Puritans. They've each taken their turns being the hero while the other plays the villain. Cristóbal Colón didn't just discover America, man. He discovered cigarettes! And the Puritans of the world have been making rules ever since!"

I was pretty sure Cristóbal was smoking something other than tobacco, but I had more important things on my mind. "Listen, the dino juice," I said.

"Si."

"Are you still interested?"

"Yeah, sure, man."

"How much will you give me for it?"

"Shit, man," Cristóbal said. "You serious?"

"Yeah, dead serious."

"Okay, okay, hang on, man." There were a few seconds of silence before Cristóbal spoke again. "How much you got?"

"A couple hundred gallons."

I could hear Cristóbal let out a whistle. "Okay, hang on." More silence. Then, "720 amero per gallon."

I took a few seconds to add it up in my head. I never did get the answer but I knew it was a lot.

"Okay," I said. "Deal."

"Call me when you get your hands on it. We'll meet at the normal spot." Cristóbal was talking about the Yadkin River at Slaters Bridge Road. We'd made a few exchanges there before. Cristóbal had picked the spot, but I knew it well from all the times my grandfather and I had waded down the river near that bridge, toting a burlap sack and feeling blindly under rocks and fallen trees for catfish to grapple out with our bare hands. I shuddered at the memory of bloodied fingers and water moccasins.

"You got it," I said to Cristóbal and hung up just as I was pulling up to Starr's apartment. It was easy to pick out which car was Starr's. The tags read: *GGGGGGGG*. G-string.

I stood outside her door for what felt like forever, working up the courage to knock. We had just fucked in a junkyard, but I was still nervous about showing up at her home uninvited. The only reason I had her address was because the Prius had added it from Starr's Halo. On one hand, I thought, had she not wanted me to know where she lived she could have blocked it. One the other hand, she didn't exactly give me her address either.

As I was deciding how to not look like a stalker, Starr's door opened.

"Ever heard of knocking?" she said. She was still wearing my t-shirt. "I've been watching you ever since you pulled up."

"I quit my job," I blurted out.

"Join the club."

I followed Starr into her apartment. It was small and didn't have a lot in it. It wasn't bad by any stretch. It certainly beat the shit out of my digs. But it made me wonder what kind of place she'd had with Brayden. She had a two-seater couch that had one cushion open and available for sitting but the other cushion served as kind of a closet for Starr's work clothes. Draped carefully across the arm and the back of the couch were various nighties, feather boas, sparkly thongs, lace top thigh highs among other stage attire. On the floor were dozens of pairs of platform pumps and zippered boots.

168

"I hope you didn't quit your job just because I don't have mine anymore," she said.

"Nah. I hated that place. Hasn't been the same since Cale sold out."

Starr cleared away some of her stripper clothes and made room for both of us to sit on the couch. She dumped most of it on the floor in a pile of elastic and lace. "I should throw all that shit away," she said.

"No," I said a little too quickly.

"Why not? It's not like I'm going to get another job dancing. Lanier was the only person in town who'd hire me. And I'm not going to wear six inch platform heels and a sequined bustier to the Piggly Wiggly."

"You could wear them for me."

"Oh yeah? What, you're going to come over to my apartment and I can dance for you, is that it? Your own private stripper. You'd like that, wouldn't you?"

"Yeah." I meant for my answer to sound sweet but I think it came out more perverted than anything. "I mean, if it was you."

"Actually, I kind of like that idea, too."

She reached down and started picking through the pile of lingerie. "What do you like?"

I scooted to the edge of the couch and started looking with her. We picked out a shimmery red one-piece number with straps that crisscrossed her belly. She took it and a pair of red knee-high boots into the bathroom and came back out a few minutes later, striking a pose as she walked to the center of her living room.

All I could say was, "Wow."

"Oh, hush."

"I mean it."

"I know you do."

She crouched at the lingerie pile again, her boots creaking, and this time we picked out a corset and matching thong, both made of gleaming black PVC. It went like this for an hour or longer, me and Starr picking out an outfit, her modeling it for me, then onto the next one. Vinyl, lace and latex. She even had a pair of boots that looked like they were made of real leather, and it made we wonder if she knew somebody like Cristóbal.

Starr had a case of Bud Light in the fridge and we got into it after about a dozen wardrobe changes. By the time we were halfway through the beer, Starr was dancing and laughing, her Halo playing the songs she danced to at Baby Dolls. She used the frame of her kitchen door like she did the pole and writhed on her living room carpet as I clapped and whistled.

After she had tried on all her work clothes, she went into her bedroom and brought out the underwear drawer from her dresser and we started working through all the things Brayden had bought for her over the years. Most of it still had the tags attached. Hot pants, stockings, push-up bras, half-bras, camisoles, teddies, nighties, negligees in cotton, satin, lace, silk and polyester. Poor Brayden had spent a small fortune on sexy things for his wife, and by her own admission, this was the first time she'd worn most of it. I almost felt bad for him.

When the Bud Light was gone and the outfits had all been modeled, Starr disappeared into her bedroom for a few minutes and came back out in a pair of jeans and my t-shirt. It was the first time I had ever seen her wearing pants. She curled up on the couch next to me and before I could chicken out, I told her that I wanted to steal Rich Boy's gasoline and sell it to Cristóbal for 720 amero a gallon and run away to Cuba with her and start a brand new life together away from all this shit.

She stared at me for a long time. The she said, "Okay."

I explained how we'd go to the junkyard after dark and round up as many gas tanks as would fit in the trunk and backseat of the Galaxie. Then I'd wire the distributor cap Cristóbal had sent and make the final preparations on the car. With any luck, the gas in the Galaxie's tank would get us out of Dugan's and to the apartments on Myers Road. We'd fill up her tank, and the others, with as much of Rich Boy's gas as we could hold, then we'd head out to meet Cristóbal.

Starr asked why we wouldn't just use the Prius. "Wouldn't it attract less attention?"

She was absolutely right, I knew, but I'd be damned if I was going to make my big getaway in a fucking Toyota Prius.

"Yeah, of course, but the cops can kill the Prius with the press of a button. They can't kill that old Galaxie. After we make the drop with Cristóbal, we'll hitch a ride on the Siluro until we get to the coast."

"What's a Siluro?"

"A catfish, I think."

"We're riding on a catfish?"

"No, it's a boat."

"We're riding on a boat?" Starr's eyes lit up.

"Yeah, Cristóbal's boat."

"Crystal ball?"

"Cristóbal. He's who we're selling the gasoline to."

"Oh."

I could tell Starr didn't understand it all, and that she didn't care. She liked the idea. That was enough.

We spent the afternoon packing up what few things Starr said she couldn't start a new life without. Mainly toiletries and a few changes of clothes. I made her pack the sequined thong she had been wearing last night when all this began. She told me she'd never been to the beach, that they never had the money for vacations growing up and Brayden had been afraid of the water. I described Varadero to her the way Cristóbal had done for me. I told her about the white sand, the turquoise water, the sun like diamonds in the waves as it rose in the morning and like flames on the water when it set. I told her how we'd swim out and wait for a wave to ride to shore, our bodies carried by the wave, our arms out before us like we were flying. And how when the wave began to break, the water would wash over us and tumble us and bounce us along the sandy slope that lead up the beach. We could lie there in the sun as the wave retreated all around us.

She asked me how many gallons I thought we could carry and I said at least a hundred. She told me that would be 72,000 amero, more than we made in a year put together. More than enough to start over.

When dark came, we left Starr's apartment and went to my trailer. I changed into my jeans and a t-shirt. I threw my Current Auto uniform in the trash. Starr helped me lift my tool chest out of the Prius and then I filled up a couple of duffle bags with the tools and threw them back in the car. I reached under the couch and pulled out Big Earl's 12-gauge, leaving it in the blanket it was wrapped in.

"Is that what I think it is?" Starr said, eying the shotgun-shaped package.

"Probably."

"I thought those things were illegal."

"So is just about everything we're going to do tonight."

"Good point," she said.

I grabbed the last slice of pickle pimento loaf from the fridge and said goodbye to the old place. I wouldn't miss it.

***

It took me and Starr about two hours to unbolt six gas tanks. We got them off an early '20s Tahoe, a 2023 Ford F-250, a trio of late '10s Explorers and 1970-something Country Squire. They all held at least twenty gallons each. After trying a few different arrangements, we were able to fit three tanks in the trunk and another three in the back seat, like some kind of puzzle. There was barely room left in the backseat for the shotgun.

Starr watched quietly as I fit the new distributor cap on and snapped each of the eight spark plug wires into place. I stood and looked at the engine for a long time, mentally going over every connection I'd made, every bolt I'd tightened over the past year on this thing. Battery; check. Water in the radiator; check. I pulled the dipstick. The oil was pure black sludge, but it would work. I snapped opened the throttle a couple of times, watching the fuel spray down the carburetor's throat. I could only hope the gas hadn't turned to varnish. I tugged on the fan belt then circled the car once, kicking each tire as I went.

Wordlessly, Starr and I got into our seats. I stared at the lifeless gauges for a while; the speedometer on *0*, fuel on *E*. All that would change soon enough.

I looked over at Starr. Her eyes were shut tight, fingers crossed on both hands, bouncing her hands off her knees.

"Here goes nothing," I whispered. I said a silent prayer to the Virgin Mary as she smiled at me serenely from her cardboard air freshener.

Starr looked between me and Mary. "Friend of yours?"

"I hope so."

I turned the key. The starter whined and ancient gears crept into motion, groaning and grinding, shuddering. I pictured flakes of ferrous rust showering the dirt beneath the engine. The engine began to spin, slowly, like an old lady pulling herself off her bed and to her feet, legs wobbly, reaching for the nightstand to brace herself. The engine spun faster, gaining strength. Crankshaft and connecting rods, cam and lifters, slowly stretched their legs and
174

limbered up until the engine was coughing, trying to ignite the gas and air that was being fed to it. A cylinder began to fire, then two. Then more. Then all eight. It sputtered and wheezed, trying to catch its breath, spitting, choking.

Then, with a bestial roar, the Galaxie came to life. I pressed the pedal to the floor and let it back off, the big 390 snarling with remembered power.

I looked at Starr, my eyes wide. "Alive, alive…" I grinned manically. "It's alive!"

She was laughing and clapping, fidgeting in her seat.

I pushed down the clutch pedal and eased the shifter into first. Then, ever so carefully, I eased the clutch out. The vines that had coiled themselves around the wheels snapped and fell away. And the car moved forward.

We crept through the junkyard, slower than a walk.

"You ever ridden in a Galaxie before?" I asked.

"Well, technically, we've been riding in a galaxy our whole lives."

"No, darling, I mean a Ford Galaxie."

"Well, in that case, no."

I listened to every sound the car made, trying to pick out any warning signs – hisses, pop, whistles, clanks or bangs – anything that indicate a problem. There was no computerized voice warning me of the perils of motor vehicles and the air I breathed. All I heard was the burble of the engine and the crunch of tires on gravel. I pulled up to the junkyard's gate and knocked her in neutral, jumping out and rounding the car, inspecting tires, head and tail lights, kneeling and looking under the engine for anything dripping. Everything looked good. Better than good.

I got back behind the wheel and Starr leaned over and planted a big kiss on my lips. I was smiling so big it almost hurt my face. I soaked it in. The sweet smell of gasoline mingling with decades-old decaying adhesives. Soft vinyl and carpet on the inside, the candy-colored shell of the body on the outside. Hot oil and metal. Organic and mechanical.

I centered the Galaxie up on the gate and backed her up a few yards. For just a moment, I almost felt bad about taking the car. But Dugan wouldn't miss one car, I told myself. Besides, after all the work I'd done to it, I figured it was mine anyhow. Squatter's rights or something. I had earned it with my busted knuckles.

Baron was sprawled out in front of the gate and I blew the Galaxie's horn once to startle him out of the way. I gunned the motor, the whole car twitching and twisting like a caged beast. Baron was crouched and cowering, watching. I tightened my grip on the wheel and popped the clutch, setting loose all of the Galaxie's power. The car lunged forward, the bellowing engine drowning out the Doberman's barks.

The front bumper crashed into the chain link gate as we charged through, severing it from the fence and sending it flipping away in front of us. I bounded onto the road, wrestling the wheel and shifter simultaneously, adrenaline surging through my veins. Out in the open now, I floored the gas pedal, the big car fishtailing and weaving.

176

I wound through second, third and then fourth gear, ignoring the speedometer. The humid night air blasted through our open windows, whipping the Virgin Mary all around. The Galaxie gathered speed, building momentum, our bodies pressed deep into the seat.

Starr let out a hoarse yell, eyes wide, smile wider, the wind lashing her hair all about her face.

It was like nothing I had ever felt before. Driving an 80-year old, 3,700 pound behemoth is not like riding in your luxury sedan in rush hour traffic. It's not like your 5-Series or 7-Series or S-Class or Q-Class or whatever nameless status symbol you've chosen for yourself. It's not like when your exit is coming up and for some reason your AutoNav has got you in the wrong lane so it drops you back a couple of car lengths to try to find somewhere to slip in line. While you sit and watch, your proximity sensors recalibrate your closing velocity and optimize your steering angle. But there's no room, so the AutoNav speeds you up, tries to get you in front of the line. Your microprocessor is frantically adjusting each wheel's 3-phase induction motors and inverters, automatically controlling your steering and braking and acceleration for you, making sure you don't exceed the posted speed limit. But that exit is coming up fast. And you grow some balls and switch back to manual control, pressing down the accelerator. 70, 75 mph now. Your continuously variable transmission struggles to keep up. 85 mph. The exit is right there. You have to get over now. You're almost clear of the lead car. You're on his front fender now. And that bastard is speeding up just to fuck with you. You're clear, so you yank the wheel and dive across two lanes, leaving juggled cups of coffee and middle fingers in your wake. God, you almost got up to 90 miles per hour. You blast through the far side of the exit lane, gravel and debris and tire crumbs scattering against the insides of your wheel wells, and for just a second you think maybe your normally sure-footed sedan might lose its precious grip on the road. But it doesn't. Your all-wheel brake-by-wire avoidance system gets you slowed down by the time you reach the top of the ramp. Your heart is pounding. You made it. Fuck yeah, you made it. God, that was fast.

Fuck you.

That wasn't fast. That wasn't shit. Take that feeling and multiply it by a factor of ten. The car I was driving lived by inhaling illegal flammable poison which it compressed and detonated in order to hurl slugs of forged steel with enough to force to cut a man in two. It was a jagged, saw-toothed beast. Its motor was a mean, unruly thing. This wasn't technology, it was machinery. Take your cabin – hermitically-sealed against airborne chemical and biological attacks – and replace it with reentry-hot air swatting your head like a boxer. Take your 8-way intuitively adjustable, lumbar supported and body temperature-reactive La-Z-Boy of a driver's seat and replace it with what amounted to a padded folding chair. A steel floor pan, a phonebook's thickness of foam cushion and a pair of Levi's were the only things separating my ass from the asphalt blurring by like a belt sander. Take the sterile silence of your lithium ion battery array and

178

replace it with the banshee howl of unrestricted internal combustion and 400 horsepower screaming down the road with a death-rattle shriek. Take your electronic throttle actuation and dynamic terrain modelling and adaptive traction control and vehicle stability control systems and get a goddamned gas pedal and a 4-speed shifter. Replace the scent of that morning's coffee with the scent of burning rubber, boiling antifreeze and spent fossil fuel; the sweet smell of countless Tyrannosaurs and Stegosaurs who gave their lives 65 million years ago so I could burn gasoline right the fuck now.

I glanced at the speedometer. 120. We were flying. I looked at Starr. In her eyes I saw the same flash of freedom I felt in my heart.

***

We only passed two other cars on our way to Myers Road, but both of them had made my heart stop until they zoomed past and I could see their taillights in the Galaxie's rearview and knew they weren't turning around to come after us. The Galaxie gave itself away from angle; its dim, round incandescent headlights from the front, her snarling exhaust note from the rear. Any cop close enough for us to spot would be close enough to us to know we were in something illegal.

We drove almost to the end of Myers Road before we found Misty Ridge Apartments.

"Oh yeah," Starr said. "I've been here before. Sapphire used to live here."

"They don't look bad enough to condemn."

"Nah, this is a shithole, trust me."

There were maybe a dozen buildings with four units each, upstairs and downstairs. More than a few apartments still had lights on even though it was close to midnight, and the parking spaces were packed with old crappy cars. I even saw a hybrid, the kind that got grandfathered in as long as you let the state disable the gas engine. I cut the Galaxie's motor and coasted, not wanting to alert the sleepy denizens of Misty Ridge to our presence.

"People still live here," I said.

Starr didn't say anything at first, then nodded to the last building in the complex. "There."

The building was dark and there were no cars parked in front of it. I steered toward it.

Slipping silently between rows of parked electrics I was struck by just how different the Galaxie was. For starters it was easily twice the size of anything else here. There was more sheet metal on one of her quarter panels than on most of these entire cars. But despite the size difference, she seemed so much sleeker. She was long and low-slung, canted into the wind. Everything from her bumpers to her windshield to her wheel wells were chrome plated. Her taillights glowed red in the dark like a pair of afterburners. Built not just for speed, but for sex appeal. The cars parked all around us were bedroom slippers. The Galaxie was a red stiletto.

180

We coasted downhill to the back of the complex. We had enough momentum to hop the curb and roll behind the apartment building, out of sight.

"Think we should leave our Halos in the car?" Starr asked.

I'd had the same thought, but then decided the cops would show up a lot quicker for a disconnected Halo than they would for a break-in. "Nah, we're better off leaving them on."

Starr and I went to the first back door we got to and tried it. Naturally it was locked but I would have felt like an idiot if had kicked in an open door.

"See anybody?" I asked Starr.

"Hunh-uh."

I stepped back and then planted my boot next to the knob as hard as I could. The door didn't budge.

"It looks easier in the movies," I said.

I kicked again, with everything I had, and this time the door surrendered with a loud crack.

I switched on my work light. We had stepped into the kitchen. The air was hot and stagnant from who knows how many August days without air conditioning.

"See?" Starr said. "Shithole."

The place was filthy. The vinyl floor was sticky in spots, slippery in others. The countertops had more splatters and stains than the floor at Cale's. I didn't even want to think about where the smell was coming from.

Starr reluctantly began going through the cabinets, opening the doors with just her fingernails, seeing nothing but empty shelves and dead flies, and then banging them shut with her elbow. She refused, so I checked the refrigerator and the oven with no luck, unless you count the blackened drippings of Lord knows what. We went upstairs and I set the light on the pock-marked carpet in the hallway, scaring away a small battalion of cockroaches and giving Starr enough light to check one bedroom while I scanned the other. There was nothing in my room except for a pile of damp and mildewed towels in the corner that looked and smelled like they had been used to dam some sort of leak. The closets and the bathroom were empty, too There was no gasoline in this apartment.

"Okay, no sweat," I said. "We weren't going to hit the jackpot right off the bat."

"At least we know why he condemned the place."

We hustled out the back door and over to the next apartment. This door gave on the first kick. Inside we found the same thing here we did in the first unit. I kicked in the back door on the other two apartments and discovered nothing but stains and roaches, some dead, most alive.

I was starting to get that feeling I got at Dugan's when I'd spent all night scouring the junkyard for a thermostat or solenoid only to get to that last row of cars and slowly realizing I wasn't going to find it. Not only had you not found what you were looking for, but there was all that wasted time and effort. It made we want to kick Rich Boy's ass all over again.

"That fucker," I finally said. "Should've known he was full of shit."

182

"Maybe he already came and got it."

"Or maybe it was never here. Maybe he was just telling you that shit to impress you."

Starr started to say something, but then seemed to consider the likelihood of what I'd just said. We stood in the kitchen of the darkened apartment a few minutes, saying nothing, until Starr finally went to the sink. "All I know is I've got to wash my hands. I feel nasty."

Before I could tell her the water was probably disconnected, I heard it splashing against the sink bowl.

Starr said, "Um, Earlie?"

"Yeah?"

"There's gasoline pouring out of the faucet."

"What?" Before I could even walk to the sink to see for myself, I could smell it. "Turn it off!"

Starr slammed the faucet handle down and stepped aside. I dragged my finger across the bottom of the bowl and held it to my nose, not that there was any doubt. The entire apartment smelled like gasoline suddenly. I turned the faucet back on and again, fuel poured out.

"What the fuck."

I stared dumbfounded for a moment before having a thought. I pushed the faucet handle over to the cold side and the gasoline stopped. I pushed it over to hot and the gas started flowing again.

"Holy shit," I said. "That fucker's filled the water heater tanks with it."

"What?"

"The gasoline is in the water heaters." I went back into the hallway and opened the tiny closet where we'd found the water heater. "Forty gallons." I knelt and opened the drain valve at the bottom of the tank. Gasoline began to flood out onto the carpet and quickly shut it off again. "Bingo."

Starr and I snuck back out to the Galaxie and carried in the first empty tank. We positioned the tank's filler neck under the water heater's drain valve and began to transfer the gasoline. It only took a couple of minutes. The full tank weighed well over a hundred pounds and it was all Starr could do to help me carry it out to the car. We carried the next empty tank in and finished off that apartment's water heater with it. Each apartment's water heater filled two gas tanks, which meant we couldn't drain the last apartment, but we didn't have room in the Galaxie anyhow.

Once we'd arranged the tanks back in the trunk and back seat, I tallied up our haul. Starr smiled at me. She might as well have had dollar signs in her eyes.

I called Cristóbal.

"We got it," I said when he answered.

"How much?"

"A hundred and twenty gallons."

"I'm in place. How long till you get here?"

"Twenty minutes max. See you then."

I fired up the Galaxie and Starr and I crept back through the apartment complex's parking lots, hoping the burbling 390 wouldn't draw too much attention until we were free and clear.

184

But apparently me kicking in doors on apartments had already done that, because about the time we got to the main road, I saw blue lights.

"Fuck." Starr said.

"Hold onto your ass," I told her.

The cop was slowing to turn off of Myers Road and into the Misty Ridge Apartments, already seeing us and angling to block our escape. I pinned the gas pedal to the floor and got there first, shooting the gap between the curb and the cop. I glanced at the passenger's side mirror just as it clipped the side mirror of the cop's vehicle and amputated it, sending it flying in a rain of glass and plastic. I saw the cop slam on the brakes and do a U-turn.

"Go, go!" Starr said.

We hit 70 mph by the time I made it to the first bend in the road. I glimpsed the flashing blue lights in the rearview as I swept through the turn, shifting gears, braking hard and then accelerating harder, speeding out into the straight.

We made it to the end of Myers Road, blowing past the stop sign, rocketing down the half-mile stretch of Elkin Highway before diving off onto Slaters Bridge Road.

In my rearview mirror I could see the black silhouette of the Brushy Mountains against the moonlit sky, rolling like sleepless-night bed sheets out of Wilkes County, down to the brown waters of the Yadkin River. It was like the Good Lord Hisself had spent millennia sanding down tall, jagged peaks with wind and rain until we were left with swells and valleys and hollers made just for snaking ribbons of faded asphalt through.

Twisting, banking roads where a man with a stout enough V8, a stiff enough set of springs and big enough set of balls could outrun prying Federal eyes, just like in the old days. Slaters Bridge Road was one of those roads. It clung to the edges of the red clay cliffs along the Yadkin River. We were close enough now to smell the silt on the wind blasting through our open windows. From the upper end, looking down toward the water, it looked like a gray snake in the moonlight, slipping silently into the river. I knew if I could make it to the bridge, that hound wouldn't catch this fox.

I watched the cop in my rearview. It was one of those freelancers; an employee of a private law enforcement contractor which provided subscription-based patrol for taxpayers fed up with a Federal government seemingly unwilling and incapable of enforcing its own rules. He rode shotgun to a computer in an electric truck called a Tactical Pursuit and Containment Vehicle. It was sheathed in ballistics-resistant composite-fiber body panels plastered with the brand logos of various corporate sponsors and suppliers which dissolved into adaptive optical camouflage when on mission. It looked like some sort of specter in my mirror, diverting the light waves around it, a transparent apparition of distorted and undulating moonlight and shadow.

Starr was watching me. "Can you outrun him?"

"You damn right."

The racks on the TPACV's grill and roof bristled with things that could stop lesser cars in their tracks; an EMP cannon, immobilization rams; deployable spike strips. None of it would

186

help him. Even if he could get close enough to use the cannon on me, it wouldn't matter. The best thing about a 1963½ Ford Galaxie 500 XL wasn't her enormous trunk that could hold over one hundred gallons. It wasn't the big V8 under her hood. It wasn't her gorgeous lines. It was the breaker points in her distributor, which were utterly impervious to electromagnetic pulses. And she couldn't be remotely shut down, either – one more reason they outlawed cars like her in the first place. Kill codes didn't exist for cars without computers, and she was built when computers didn't drive a man's car for him. She was built when you needed to know how to do things like accelerate and steer and brake.

Seventy miles an hour Slaters Bridge Road was fast. 80 mph was palms sweating fast. 90 mph was your pulse like a kettle drum in your head fast. 100 mph was tunnel vision and your peripheral smeared. Factor in the 115 gallons of Lanier Morse's gasoline I was carrying in the trunk, and the 700 pounds it added to the Galaxie's already hefty 3,700, and the focus it took to keep from accidentally killing myself at that speed was exhausting. 100 mph was what it would to take to get to the river before the cop did.

I scanned the asphalt with radar eyes, making sure the potholes and corrugations were exactly where I remembered. I listened through the whine of the gears and the howl of the engine, just like Daddy had taught me, picking out the important sounds; lifters and rockers, valves, jets and secondaries. My hands gripped the wheel, sensing every bearing and spring shackle, the vibrations and tugs telling me what the road was doing beneath me. The air whistled in through the gaps and it smelled like burning asbestos and river bed; my nose told me if the fuel mixture was too rich or too lean. My spit tasted like a mouthful of pennies, letting me know I was just scared enough. The speed of the car became secondary to the speed of everything else that was happening; the speed at which the bridge was approaching. The speed of my reflexes. The speed of fear.

I hurtled down Slaters Bridge Road, diving into a curve, gearing down, braking, sawing the wheel, back in the gas, accelerating hard. I knew the cop was lighting me up with his on-board thermal targeting laser, which instantly relaying my coordinates to a satellite 10,988 nautical miles above me where my heat/emissions signature and telemetry was being spectrally analyzed in geosynchronous orbit. I also knew he wouldn't be allowed to exceed Federally mandated pursuit risk parameters.

The bridge was less than a mile away. We hadn't lost our hound yet. I thought for a minute about pulling the 12-gauge from the backseat and having Starr spray a couple of Pheasant loads against the revenuer's shatter-proof windshield.

We had to slow for an S-turn and just like that the TPCAV's adaptive traction control launched the truck beside me without so much as a chirp from its non-pneumatic tires. He was on us instantly. I slammed the shifter into second. The hood of the Galaxie flashed under the moonlight that strobed through the treetops. We streaked down the road side by side.

The TPACV veered, slamming into us with a deafening crash, throwing me against the door and Starr across my lap. Our vehicles scraped and struggled against one another, the cop trying to force me into the ditch but not having enough weight or power to do so. The Galaxie's right-side tires slid off the pavement for just a moment, spraying a sleet of gravel against the fenders like buckshot before we muscled our way back onto the road. I could see the scoring and gouges the Galaxie's steel body had left in the TPACV's composite-fiber panels. Its damaged LED unit was now aimed down at the pavement like a lazy eye.

I looked over at the cop. The moon shone across his face. He was waving frantically for me to pull over, as if I hadn't gotten the hint. Starr leaned up to look, too, and then she said, "Holy shit."

I looked at her, then back at the cop. His mouth had hung open and he was staring at Starr like he'd seen a ghost. Then he mouthed something that looked an awful lot like, "Cassie?"

"You know him?" I yelled over the roar of the motor.

Before she could answer, the cop had rammed into us again, this time sending my back tires skipping across the pavement. I stood on the gas, holding the throttle wide open. And we started pulling away. It was like we'd fired a retrorocket or something. Like we'd flipped a switch. Then I realized we weren't going any faster, it was the TPACV that was slowing down. I watched its lights shrink in my rearview mirror until they finally blinked out around a bend.

"Of course!" There was a huge smile on Starr's face. "The coronal mass ejection!"

"The what?"

"The geomagnetic storm," she said. "Didn't you get the update?"

I remembered suddenly. Like I did with most of the bullshit the Prius said, I had all but ignored it at the time. Starr excitedly described to me how a coronal mass ejection was an ejection of electrons and protons from the sun, and how when it reaches the Earth it can fuck with our magnetosphere, causing power outages and disputing radio transmissions. All that mattered to me was that the cop was gone.

"It can even knock out satellites," she explained. And then I got it. The cop was adrift without his GPS, and the TPACV had been automatically shut down.

"So, this storm must have..."

"Exactly!" She squealed and gave me a big hug. She popped out of her seat and hung her body out the passenger's side window, perching on the door and yelling back into the night. "Fuck you, Brayden! Who's the bitch now?"

She dropped back into her seat, clapping and laughing. I couldn't help but laugh with her. Then it hit me.

"Brayden?"

"That was him."

"No shit?"

"No shit." Then she started giggling at the thought of having just outrun her husband.

The bridge was just ahead. I scanned the roadside, watching for the nearly invisible gap hidden in the rhododendrons that marked the entrance to the rutted trail that lead down to the river where Cristóbal would have the Siluro tied off.

I spoke his name into my Halo, calling him to let him know we were almost there.

"Won't work," Starr said. "If the storm knocked out Brayden's GPS, it will have knocked out the phones, too."

She was right, Cristóbal didn't answer. The entrance to the trail appeared and I stood on the brakes and geared down, letting the drag of the engine help cut my speed in half. I dove off the pavement and slipped through the roadside hedge, the Galaxie seemingly swallowed up by the woods.

I'd made this trip before, picking up items that Cristóbal didn't trust mailing. The Galaxie's battery, a quart of gear oil and the fuel filter among the things I'd taken possession of directly. We glided through the foliage, the trail barely as wide as the car, tree branches dragging along our fenders like skeletal fingers. We plowed through ruts, mowing down saplings and vaulting over roots and ridges. The beams of our headlights shot all around; down at the vine-carpeted forest floor below and then into the canopy.

I let the Galaxie coast to a stop well short of the waterline, before the tires began to sink in the riverbank mud. I climbed out and listened for the sound of the TPACV sneaking down the trail behind me, but all I heard was the crickets, frogs and the constant babbling of the water, all accompanied by the incessant call of a lone whippoorwill.

The Siluro was beached on the clay, the water slapping against its wooden hull.

"Que pasa, pendejo!" Cristóbal was wading out of the river next to his boat.

We shook hands but he had already lost interest in me, his eyes moving up and down Starr.

"Cristóbal, this is my—" I almost called her my girlfriend but chickened out. "Starr."

"Ah," Cristóbal nodded with an appreciative smile. "Muy romántico to call one's lady an estrella."

"No, her name—"

"I think I will use that on my Carmela," he said. "You mind?"

Starr said, "My name is Starr." She took Cristóbal's hand and shook it.

"Ah, I see," he said. "And you are as a beautiful as one."

I could only roll my eyes. "We might need to get this show on the road. We had company a couple miles back."

"Police?"

"Yeah. We lost him, but we don't need to fuck around, neither."

I opened the Galaxie's cavernous trunk began hauling out the tanks with Cristóbal's help.

"So listen," I said. "You got room for a couple of stowaways?"

192

"Que?"

"Me and Starr. We need a ride to the beach."

Cristóbal watched me for a second, making sure I was serious. Then he said, "Rides ain't free, my friend."

"I understand. How about you keep one of these tanks for fare?"

Cristóbal did the math in his head. At 720 amero a gallon, a full tank would be worth close to 15 grand for a trip he was making anyhow.

He began to nod. "Si, si. You got a deal."

As he and I went back to the car to extract the last tank, we were suddenly drenched in white light. In the woods, a jostling spotlight was being held on us. Cristóbal crouched behind the bumper of the Galaxie. I duck-walked around the car and looked for Starr. She was already in the boat, peering at me over the hull. I motioned for her to get down and stay put.

"Don't move!" came a voice from the woods.

Cristóbal was splashing into the river, lifting himself into the boat.

"Freeze!" the voice called again. "You're under arrest!"

Cristóbal had started yanking on the cord of the ancient Evinrude perched on the stern of the Siluro. I could see Brayden's silhouette now, the spotlight held out in front of him, aimed at me. I thought about charging him and buying some time for Cristóbal and Starr, but the last thing I needed was assault to go along with my possession of petroleum products with intent to distribute, a count of operation of an internal combustion engine, evading, a slew of firearms charges, not to mention having Starr mad at me for kicking her ex-husband's ass.

The boat's motor suddenly coughed to life.

"Come on!" I heard Starr yell.

I looked at Cristóbal and said, "Don't wait on me."

"No, come on!" Starr called out.

"I'll catch up with you. I'll meet you at the next bridge." It was bullshit, but Starr seemed to believe it.

My mind was racing with potential escape plans, and just as quickly I formulated each plan's faults. There was no way for me to get away, but at least Starr and Cristóbal could. I watched Brayden as he closed in on me, easing aside a low-slung branch with one hand, holding the other up to me to show me that he was unarmed. He stepped cautiously toward the car, both hands out now, a look on his face that seemed to say, "Nice doggie."

I stepped away from the car and waited. Brayden's gaze shifted from me to the Galaxie.

"Whatcha got in it?" he said. It took me a moment to realize he was asking about the engine, not the contraband that had been in the trunk.

I could see the Siluro easing out into the deep part of the water. Brayden paid it no attention. Wordlessly I raised the Galaxie's hood, revealing the big V8 beneath, the heat rolling out in waves. His eyes flashed with excitement. "390. Holley four-barrel. High-rise intake. Nice." He stared some more before speaking again.

"You know, Cassie always used to say there were three kinds of cops." He was looking at me now. "There was the guy who simply thought being a cop would be cool. He thought it would be fun to have a patrol car and a gun. Thought he'd look good in a uniform. Wanted to catch the bad guys and play cops and robbers. But at the end of the day, it was just a job. Cass said that's what kind of cop I was. She used to say that I could have just as easily been a manager at the bank had they called for an interview before the security contractor did."

I could hear her saying exactly that. Brayden seemed to be waiting on me to say something, but all I did was nod and watch the Siluro disappear into the darkness.

Brayden said, "Cassie said the second kind of cop was the guy who truly wanted to serve and protect. The kind of cop who understood his duty was to simply enforce the laws, not interpret them or pass judgment, moral or otherwise. This kind of cop was the rarest of all, according to her. When I'd told her that was the kind of cop I thought I was, she'd just laugh."

Cristóbal and Starr were gone now. I couldn't even hear the motor anymore.

Brayden kept talking, leaning under the hood now, pointing his spotlight at anything with chrome on it. "Cass said the third kind of cop was the worst kind. The scary kind. The kind who had an axe to grind. A chip on his shoulder. Maybe he had been bullied in school. Been on the wrong end of more than his share of atomic wedgies. Maybe one too many girls had rejected him. He might have been a little on the short side. A little chubby, maybe. And it all had made him more than a little mean. But he knew if he could get through the training, then he could turn the tables. He'd have a badge. And a billy stick. The full weight of the law on his side. Not to mention the benefit of the doubt when any judge or jury was asked to take his word over someone else's. He'd be the one with the power now."

Brayden finally turned and looked down the river. There was nothing to see. "When we'd fight, which was often, Starr would accuse me of not being able to admit when I was wrong. It was part of my training, she'd say. Cops were supposed to be infallible. A cop couldn't ever say he'd made a mistake."

I watched Brayden for a minute, ready for him to cuff me. Instead he said, "Tell Cass I made a mistake. Tell her I'm sorry. Tell her I'm sorry for being the third kind of husband."

And with that he turned and disappeared into the dark woods. I stood and waited until I couldn't hear his footsteps in the leaves anymore. After a few minutes I could see the lights of his TPACV up on Slaters Bridge Road, driving away. As I slipped behind the wheel of the Galaxie and eyed the jasmine-scented Virgin Mary, ready to ask for some timely assistance, I saw a flashing light on the river. By the time I got the water's edge, Cristóbal and Starr had paddled the Siluro silently onto the bank.

We loaded the last gas tank onto the boat. I said a thank-you and goodbye to the Galaxie and left her where she sat. Starr and I threw our Halos in the river. I waited for her to ask what her husband had said to me, but when it became clear she wasn't going to, I told her anyhow. I didn't even change any of it. She didn't have a whole lot to say about it.

By the time the sun rose, the three of us were at the confluence of the Yadkin and the Uwharrie, where we slept under the sweet gum trees and waited for the sun to go away again.

When I woke at dusk, Starr was gone. Cristóbal handed me a hand-written note. He couldn't look at me.

Earlie,

First off, thank you for making me feel worth running away with. Thanks for the ride in your Galaxie. (and I'm not just talking about the backseat...ha-ha...) Secondly, I'm sorry. I know you don't understand. But I can't do this. I have to give him another chance. He's not a bad guy. I hope you could see that. I guess I'll have to wait a while longer to see the ocean. I hope you find what you're looking for. Good luck.

Love,
Starr

I sat and watched the black water slip by the hull of the boat. Cristóbal and I didn't talk for a while. I wanted to ask him what Starr had said when she left, how she was going to get back home, if she had seemed okay.

When Cristóbal finally spoke, he told me Starr had made the right decision for her and I was making the right decision for me. I wanted to tell him he was full of shit, but he was only trying to help. For a long time I weighed the consequences of going back and finding her, telling her she belonged with me. But I wasn't sure she really did. And I didn't want to go to jail or back to work at Cale's, and I knew I'd have to do one or the other.

By the next sunrise, Cristóbal and I were halfway down the Pee Dee. By the next, we were in Winyah Bay, where we transferred the gas tanks onto the Mantarraya. The boat was fast as hell, but it was still a seventeen hour ride. We never saw the Coast Guard. Along with 120 gallons of American gasoline we arrived in Cuba, where the automobile and the economy at large still ran on petroleum, despite sanctions from the North American Union. I let Cristóbal keep the gas and he let me stay with him and Carmela and little Cristóbal for a while.

***

I wrote a letter. A few months later I got up the nerve to mail it.

Dear Starr,

I'm mailing this to your old address even though I know you don't live there anymore. Hopefully it will get forwarded and find you. I would've tried your Halo but I don't have one anymore. So I'm using old-fashioned pen and paper. I'm sorry I haven't written until now but I didn't know what to say. So instead I took some pictures.

The first one is me, taken by Manuel, my new boss (more on him in just a second). I haven't been to the barber since you last saw me. My hair is almost as long as it was before Brayden Podner made me cut it.

The second picture is me and Manuel at Calle 25 Mecánico, where I work. I'm turning wrenches on all the old Detroit iron that clogs the streets of Havana. You wouldn't believe how many American cars are down here. I mean real cars, with actual engines. Manuel looks so happy because he's never had a mechanic would could read the repair manuals before. (they're in English)

The next picture is me and Cristóbal's son, Cristóbal. He is teaching me Spanish. I'm not very good yet. The picture was taken in the room I rent in Vedado. It's got a balcony but it's not close enough for me to see the ocean. I asked Cristóbal to bring me a telescope from the States, but I can't even see Cassiopeia because of all the city lights. So me and Cristóbal drive out to the country sometimes and look through my telescope at the beautiful upside-down queen.

The fourth picture is my new girlfriend, Estrella. She's a '65. Galaxie, of course. Signal Flare Red. She's got a 289 that runs pretty good, but it's a boat anchor compared to the 390 that was in our 63 ½. She beats the shit out of my Prius, though.

I think about you a lot. I hope you're happy. I know that sounds smartass, but I mean it. You were mine for less than 24 hours, but it was better than nothing.

If you're ever in Cuba, look me up. I'll be the gringo riding in the Galaxie.

Love,

Earlie

Coda

That bank of the Yadkin River was the final resting place for the 60 millionth Ford ever built.

In its first winter, an early ice storm broke a limb off an ash tree overhead. The limb shattered the Galaxie's windshield.

The following spring, a mother raccoon gave birth to four kits in the floorboard amidst the leaves and branches that had fallen into the car. For the rest of the summer, the young raccoons came and went, gamboling across the front seat and dash and hood.

A father and son on a fishing trip saw the car from their canoe and stopped and took the hood ornament as a keepsake.

A maple seed fell through the cowl vent, through a rusted out hole in the firewall, down through the engine compartment and into the soft, fertile soil. It took hold and became a sapling, growing slowly, surely, until it pushed open the hood and stretched up toward the canopy.

A young couple on a hike made love on a blanket in the back seat during a rain storm.

At one point, the river spilled over its banks and the car was partially submerged. A catfish got caught in a pool in the floorboard and died when the river receded.

The tires deflated within a few years, although the rubber they were made of stayed intact for centuries.

The paint deteriorated quickly, and once it flaked away, rust began to ravage the unprotected sheet metal until only a skeleton of the car remained.

Moss and vines that had been climbing onto the body for decades began to pull the car down into the ground, like zombie fingers pulling a victim into the grave.

After a century, the Galaxie was a barely recognizable heap of slumping metal. Iron and steel reverted back to the minerals they came from.

Ashes to ashes, dust to dust.

Scream If You Wanna Go Faster

Wade Beauchamp

Scream If You Wanna Go Faster

Wade Beauchamp

Scream If You Wanna Go Faster